ISBN: 979-8-9852062-2-7

This is a work of fiction. Names, characters, business, events and incidents are the products of the author's imagination. Any resemblance to actual persons, living or dead, or actual events is purely coincidental.

Cover Design by: Isu Designs
Interior Design by: Isu Designs

First printing edition 2024.

Pondicherry Books
www.pondicherrybooks.webnode.com

Rifts

David Mansell

PONDICHERRY BOOKS

RIFTS

DAVID MANSELL

1
POLLUTION

At night the office was oppressively quiet. The huge open room, normally full of people was almost completely empty. The harsh lighting really only demonstrated the blackness of the surrounding night, a cube of shrill white completely enclosed by still, inky mystery. The only sounds were the air heaters occasionally kicking in, or the muted sound of distant traffic.

One man sat at his desk, staring at his phone. His large frame sat easily in the office chair, although he was wary of moving too quickly in it. The cautionary groans whenever he played with the flappy paddle under the seat were a constant reminder that he was not losing his weight. His mind, as ever, taunted him in his moment of reflection.

Almost as if you don't do any .... fit thing.
Nice.
You don't even know the right words to be healthy.
Idiot.
You're so lucky you have a girlfriend.

Geoff grinned as he watched and waited. He had sent off a text only minutes before to his lady, Emily. He was quite sure she would write him soon. Today was their third month anniversary. He was sorry that he had to work but his boss had made it clear Geoff was already on thin ice. Geoff was notoriously late, a situation made all the worse due to his house being so close to work. Trying to get back into the boss's good books, Geoff had volunteered for the night shift. Now all alone for the next six hours, Geoff was looking forward to a quiet night. His job handled water maintenance. During the day, the office would be inundated with emails and phone calls, asking for engineers to attend blocked toilets, or showers with low pressure. At night, there would normally be only one or two calls. Geoff was hoping for no problems the whole night. He wanted to settle down with his phone for the night.

No coworkers.
No boss.
Just you, and your lady.

Hours passed. Geoff had put his phone down, but kept giving it sidelong glances. Emily had not yet replied, and it was now one hour to the end of his shift. Geoff yawned, feeling the sleep in his eyes pushing into his eyelids from the stretched motion.

Coffee.

He got up and padded over to the kitchen area, a crowded, loud room he avoided during normal working hours. Pouring himself a large mug, he came back to his desk and refreshed his screen.

Shit.

Geoff sighed as he looked at his computer screen. It was an ugly animation of flashing red messages and the symbols that showed up on the map were not good at all. The computer was a principal element of the sewage response team. It received every call about sewage problems. These would range from a blocked toilet to a mainline burst. POL1 was featuring very heavily on Geoff's screen at the moment. In fact, it was becoming easier to see where there wasn't a POL1 on the screen. Geoff looked closer at the information. Four mains had simultaneously burst, a heretofore unprecedented event, and they were pouring into the River Thames. There was little Geoff could do about it.

2

Geoff sighed and reached for the telephone again. There were only so many vehicles designed to deal with such a heavy pollution. The government, in its infinite wisdom of auctioneering the area to private contractors, had chosen a company who had made promises to be competent at the lowest price possible. This had resulted in the smallest number of sewage trucks available at any one time and having them spread over a very wide area. It also meant there was an onus on the computer operator to convince the truck driver to get up at five in the morning.

"Gary, you need to get over to Reading now."

"Nah mate, I don't think I can. I am feeling a bit rough, know what I mean?"

"I don't. I don't know what you mean. I know you're meant to be on shift right now and you are the only truck operational that can handle it."

"Look, it'll take me forty-five minutes to get there. Mikey starts his shift in ninety minutes and he lives much closer. Why don't you just leave it until then, eh?"

"There is sewage pouring out of a pipe and going into the river as we speak. Gallons of toxins, all going into the home of animals and birds, all of whom are going to die. Not to mention the government who will probably fine us into oblivion. This is not going to be a job one truck can handle."

"Then why are you telling me to go out there alone?"

"Because Mikey will join you in ninety minutes, and he can help you. But you need to get out there now before the whole river dies of pollution."

"Nah, I'm not doing it. I'll think about maybe going down there later. Maybe." The phone clicked.

Don't shout.
Don't throw the phone.

Don't.
Just don't.

He carefully put the phone down. He breathed slowly. He looked around the empty office. His manager was not coming in for another three hours. Geoff looked at his watch. His shift would finish in an hour. He paused for a moment, letting his thoughts unjumble themselves. The early hour made him wince at such mental exercise.

He pulled over the Post-It Notes and wrote a note to the next person who would come on shift to contact Mikey and to check up on Gary. His handwriting was normally a decent level of calligraphy but it was a little too early in the day for that sort of thing. Besides, he was not sure how well his replacement could read. This was not the sort of place that attracted the cream of the crop. It was the lack of talent that enabled Geoff to get the job in the first place. Mikey and Gary were perfect examples of this. Having the ability to drive a big rig was a skill to be sure, but that was the extent of the drivers' knowledge or skillset.

Unfortunately, as the only two drivers of the big rigs, vehicles with enough power to fix the POL1s that were leaping about on his screen, they kept the rigs near their homes. This gave them the opportunity to get to problems quickly. It also meant when they did not, problems mounted up. Geoff looked at his note and then at his screen worriedly. By this time the whole screen was a mess of flashing red and beeping sounds. The note did explain why the calls were going unanswered but it did not solve the situation. He just hoped it would be enough. He leaned back, breathed out slowly and looked at the clock on the wall.

Geoff held the landline in his hands, the dull tone entering his brain and breaking into splinters. He thought about which subcontractor to ring at this time of night.

His mobile beeped loudly.

Emily!

He swung round quickly to the source of the sound, landline handset still in hand. The wire brushed across the table and neatly flipped the

4

steaming coffee cup. He watched it rise up impossibly slowly, before it crashed over the lip of the cup.

NO!

The coffee flew across the table and the keyboard, covering it. The liquid cascaded down the back of the desk. Sparks flew as it hit the power source. Geoff's screen went blank.

NO!

Geoff stared at the blank screen, his reflection lit up by the neon expanse. He ducked down and stared at the rear of his desk. The whole thing looked fried. He looked down at the still, silent metal box for a moment. Geoff slowly pushed his desktop box power button. Nothing happened. He looked at the other desks. He wasn't allowed to use anyone else's computer, the individual password system forcing everyone to work from their desk only, even if the signed declaration of intent to protect information had not sufficiently cowed you. He stared stupidly around the office, wishing someone else was there. He got up slowly, and pulled a large length of tissue from the canteen. Returning to his desk and slowly mopping up the coffee, Geoff tried not to think of the sewage pouring into the River Thames as he knelt there. The guilty thought crept into his mind unbidden.

One more hour until someone comes.
Then you can go home to your lady.
Emily!

Geoff's eyes widened as he remembered. He got up too quickly and hit the back of his head on the underside of the desk. Quietly cursing to himself, he staggered back into his chair and reached for his phone.

Probably should have put your boss's number on here.
Also, office coworkers.

Geoff opened the message.

Sorry, it's not working out. I hope you are happy, or whatever. Any way you want it! E.

5

Geoff furrowed his brow as he reread it. Again and again and again, the words making no sense, their fonts twisting into laughing hyenas, dancing through his eyes. Even as he sought to comprehend, he already knew a part of him was having a sullen celebration.

What?
You KNEW this was going to happen!
You KNEW it!
She was never going to stay with you. Look at you!
She lied.
Woman are a ruse.
Any way you want it.
What does that mean?
What?
What does it even mean!

Geoff shook his head furiously, the tears announcing themselves on his cheek. He stared at his dead screen, a blurry reflection made blurrier by more tears. He gripped his mobile tightly, half hoping it would be crushed by the pressure of his whitened knuckled grip. He nodded imperceptibly to himself.

Any way you want it.

He wrote a message on a series of Post-It Notes and stuck them on his computer.

Computer died.
Phone died.
Pollution in Thames.
Sorry.
Geoff.

He got up, stumbled out of the office and went home. It would be an hour before anyone else would be in the office. Hopefully, by then he would be asleep.

One more hour to go.

The light behind him, Geoff stumbled out into the darkness to his house.

Three and a half hours later, Geoff was in bed fast asleep when the phone rang. He answered it, knowing it could only be his boss ringing him at seven. The conversation was quick and to the point. By the end of the call, Geoff was fired. Geoff held the phone numbly in his hand as he lay in his bed, staring unseeingly at the ceiling. The birds were singing and the sun was shining through his window and he was unemployed.

Apparently the news media had got hold of the story. Video footage of sewage leaking, pouring really, into the local river had made the early morning news, which meant short of a bigger disaster occurring, it would be the number one story for the day. Geoff pulled his laptop off the floor, dragging through the debris in his room, and looked at the footage. He winced. His boss, his former boss, had been absolutely right to be raging. Geoff idly wondered if Gary or Mikey were also fired. He decided probably not. They were important, vital to his company. If Geoff knew one thing in this world, he was not.

He got out of bed and went to the kitchen. His mum and dad were up already of course, a lifetime of work forcing their body clock to wake early even if they were now both retired. His dad was munching on a piece of marmite and toast, looking at the little yellow TV they kept in the kitchen. The news was playing the same footage again. It had been, what, five minutes? His mum was still making the coffee.

"Hello, dear," said his mother in a surprised tone. "I thought you were still asleep."

"My boss just rang."

"Oh yes. Anything wrong?" The edge in his mother's tone rankled. She carefully placed her hands on the counter and looked at Geoff.

"He fired me. It wasn't my fault but there was a massive pollution last night-"

"This was you? Amazing. Your screw-ups are making the national news. You should be proud." The bark of his father whose position had

7

not shifted from the TV was a blow to Geoff's gut. His dad always knew exactly what to say to make Geoff feel like jumping off a bridge. It didn't help that the things said were, in some deep dark part of his soul that he didn't want to contemplate too much, totally being agreed with.

"Yup. I don't know, I guess I'm not so good with customer services." Geoff often thought his dad looked like a rugby playing accountant. The truth was, his dad had worked every day of his life in his own business up until his retirement. The fact that he was not able to perform to the same standard had been the subject of much uncomfortable discussion. His dad looked at him, his eyes dancing over the edge of his glasses.

"Sit down, Geoff."

"Dad, please, I am not in the mood for another one of your-"

"What? What did I say? Just sit down."

"Fine." Geoff sat down slowly, his hands raised in defeat before slowing bringing them down to the table.

"Your mother and I think you are not happy at the moment. You can't find a job you like for more than three months. You don't have a girlfriend. You don't seem to have anything going on."

Thank you for that.

"Sorry I am not up to current standard, Dad."

"Don't be rude. Your father is trying to help you." The admonition from his mother quietened Geoff. She brought the coffee pot over and sat down next to his father. They held each other's hands.

"Now, you've made the news. You're probably as toxic as what's coming out of there. All I am saying is maybe you are not looking for the right kind of job. What do you want to do?" His father's questioning face made Geoff wince.

"I don't know."

"What do you like doing?"

"I don't know." Geoff shrugged his shoulders helplessly at his parents.

"You liked being a youth leader, didn't you?"

I liked mucking about with kids for pocket money.
Not really a career choice.

"I don't think you can do that for a living."

"Kids. You like kids. You're good with them." The judgement having been made, his father poured himself some coffee. He sipped at it for a moment and sat back. Mum and Geoff waited expectantly. The stiff-backed man took another sip, then put the cup down. He started to smile. Seeing the smile, Geoff's mother started to smile as well. Her man had come up with another brilliant idea. Geoff groaned inwardly.

Wonderful.
Another life-changing idea.
Which, of course, I'll take.
Any way you want it, father.

"I have a friend. He left England twenty years ago. He moved to South Korea and became a teacher. He didn't know how to teach and he said it wasn't important. All you need is a degree and you have that.

In Hotel Management.

"They pay for your flight, they pay you a good wage. You can live like a king out there, he said. I don't know about that, but I know you can't stay here anymore. We have been carrying you for too long. Mother, go get his passport. Geoff, get on that internet and look up TEFL teaching in Korea."

The next twenty four hours became a blur to Geoff. Finding and applying for a job would normally take days or weeks. Employers would want one or two face to face interviews, references, proof of stated skillsets. That was not the case here. The first place he applied to online phoned him back five minutes later. The phone call turned out to be a job interview. Geoff stumbled through it, his parents watching from the doorway. By the end of the conversation he had received an email confirming his flight ticket. His mother packed his bags for him and his dad drove him to the airport.

By the time he was in the departure lounge, Geoff was thoroughly shell shocked. On Sunday he was working as a Pollutions Response Team member and was responsible for the largest pollution in London for a decade. By Monday his face was on the front page with the headline IS THIS THE MOST DANGEROUS MAN IN ENGLAND? The check-in counter attendant gave him a look indicating mild interest at a mild celebrity. By Tuesday he was leaving to become a TEFL teacher in South Korea. Geoff had no idea how to be a teacher but he had seen the steely eyed focus of his parents.

I can go anywhere, but I can't live here.

2
TRACKS

Ninety days later, Geoff had only slightly adjusted to his new life. His sole points of contact were Mr. and Mrs. Kim. They were a couple in their forties and ran his school, or *hagwan*. Mr. Kim was a thin, lantern faced man who liked to smoke thin cigarettes out of the side of his mouth. Mrs. Kim was a powerfully built woman, with short hair and a penchant for tracksuits. They spoke English passably well. At least, they were able to communicate ideas to Geoff and he understood them. When Geoff had a problem, they didn't seem to understand as well.

Geoff certainly had had some problems. On his first day, suffering mightily from jet lag, he was shown his apartment from the front door step. From what he could see, it was the smallest one-room apartment in the history of civilization. There was black mold spotting on one of the faded lurid pink flowered wallpaper walls, which the Director assured him was not a problem, and the toilet appeared to be in the shower. Then he was whisked away to the school. Geoff had seen proper schools as they drove, large buildings, fenced off with dusty football fields, filled with uniformed boys and girls. However, he was to work in a *hagwan*. These after school academies were considered an essential part of a child's education. Those who had a lot of money could send their children to the best *hagwans*. For those who did not have as much money, there were a host of chain *hagwans*. For those who had even less money, there was Geoff's academy.

11

'Happy Happy Joy Joy school for Little Genuses.'

Geoff had spotted the spelling mistake and pointed it out to Mr. Kim. Mr. Kim just smiled and nodded and repeatedly said the word geniuses. The building itself was a nondescript old building. There were ten floors. The first floor was a bank. The second floor was a doctor's office. The third floor was a café. The fourth to seventh floors were a mystery. The eighth floor was a now closed dance studio. The top two floors were the school. However, only the ninth floor was used by the school. The top floor was only accessible by a set of stairs within the school's main floor. Geoff's classroom was located on this otherwise derelict floor. Students had to walk down a dusty corridor, with chipped paint on the walls, and flickering fluoro tubes lighting the way. Geoff's classroom had a window facing out over the city. However, it was painted shut and the outside was so dirty there was no view available.

Geoff liked the solitude. He could walk into work, go into his classroom, spend the full day there, and then leave without ever seeing his bosses or any of the other teachers. After the first day, where he had been introduced to the other teachers, no one had come to speak to him. To be fair, Geoff had not deigned to speak to any of them either. He was not sure if they even spoke English.

His apartment was not pleasant. It smelled bad; the mold was probably responsible. His bed had clean sheets but the springs were broken. He would always wake up with a bad back. When he mentioned it to Mr. Kim he found out 'back pain' was one of those phrases, like 'moldy wall', or 'little geniuses', that Mr. Kim did not understand.

The bathroom consisted of a shower head attached to the sink, and a toilet seat directly opposite. It was impossible for Geoff to brush his teeth or wash his face without sitting down on the toilet. The shower would constantly drip onto the toilet seat. Geoff learned to accept taking a dump would lead to a wet bum if he was not paying attention.

The kitchen had one spoon, one knife, one fork, one bowl, one plate, and one glass. Cooking food in the apartment was fine; eating by himself in a room filled with his favourite music coming out of his tiny computer speakers was satisfying. It was far better than ordering out.

Most restaurants did not have an English menu nor any staff who spoke English. Finally, after two weeks Geoff found a restaurant that had pictures of food. He pointed at one of the pictures to the older woman, or *ajumma,* behind the counter.

"*Bibimbap?*" asked the friendly, smiling *ajumma.*

"Yep, sure, that, yep, yes, yes please," said Geoff and sat down. When the food arrived, it was a set of vegetables neatly sliced, placed over a bed of rice. The *ajumma* placed it on the table and cocked her head at the young man. Geoff looked at her confused. She smiled and pointed at the food.

"Bibimbap?"

"If you say so, I mean, I don't know."

"Bibimbap?"

Geoff put up his hands up in manic confusion. The *ajumma* started forward and grabbed Geoff's bowl. She jammed a spoon into the food and mixed it about. Then she added some sauce, and mixed it again. When she handed it back to Geoff there was a victorious glint in her eye.

"Bibimbap," and she turned and went back to the kitchen. Geoff shrugged and tried it. It was a little salty, and a little spicy, and really quite delicious. He turned to the woman and gave her a thumbs up. She smirked and nodded and pointed to the food.

"Bibimbap."

"Bibimbap."

Well done, you've just started learning Korean.

After that, the restaurant became one of the regularities in Geoff's life. Still, things remained wildly confusing in Korea. He didn't know almost any other part of the city. He took a subway to the centre of the city and wandered around. It took him about an hour to find another station to

13

get back home. He found a market once but he preferred the convenience store just down the road from him. The fresh seafood in the market looked too fresh -- their slow, ponderous swimming in the tiny plastic bucket reminding him of languidly unfolding lava he'd once seen on TV.

Plus you can't cook without printed instructions.

As for fun, Geoff spent most of his time inside his low ceilinged apartment. When he ventured out at night he went to a local dive called In My Memory. This was a favoured haunt of the expat community, at least in Geoff's neighbourhood. It was a ground floor bar, with comfortable chairs and subtle lighting. One wall was filled with old vinyl records. Everywhere else was tastefully decorated with vintage memorabilia. It certainly made for a break from all the neon and cutesy cartoon characters most Korean bars felt obliged to force on their clientele. Geoff had first found the place when he had noticed a group of white people walking into the bar. He had followed them, full of plans to introduce himself and form lifelong friends with them all. The night had passed with the group laughing uproariously, having a great time. Geoff had been at the bar by himself, nursing a series of weak Korean beers. After the shame of the pollution incident, he just could not find the strength to put himself on the line. His time in Korea had thus been spent in self-enforced solitary exile. The bar owner served him and left him alone.

He felt like a ghost most of the time in there. He watched the foreigners have their fun, night after night. He watched the Koreans come in, either as groups of businessmen, or couples looking for an exotic experience surrounded by foreigners.

Geoff had never been a fan of misogyny back in England; the cavemen who treated their partners like they were underlings had irritated Geoff a lot. Seeing how Korean men would pull their ladies along by the forearm raised Geoff's hackles. He would grimace and turn back to the bar.

Don't get involved.
It always ends badly.
You don't want any more trouble.
Women.

He was not good with women and generally felt suspicious, as if they were all part of a larger ruse to make him look like a fool. In his lifetime, there had only been two women he truly loved and one of them was his mother. The other had not turned out …. well.

So his time in Korea went. He kept himself to himself, and no one would bother him.

Time served.
Any way you want it.

As he walked into work that chilly morning, Geoff dodged the usual array of obstacles in his path.

Rubbish bags.
Old lady, mind the elbows.
Four school girls walking arm in arm.
Old man selling chestnuts on the side of the road.
Don't tread on his nuts.
Heh. Nuts.
Old lady.
Another old lady.
Another old lady.
Where are all the old men?
Oh there. There's one.
He's drinking soju at eight in the morning.
Probably why there aren't a lot of old men.

He got to his dilapidated building and jogged up the stairs. As he entered the school, he waved at Mr. Kim.

"Morning," said the Englishman.

Mr. Kim frowned at Geoff and grabbed his forearm.

Well this can't be good.

The director pulled the unresisting excuse of a teacher up the inner stair and along the corridor.

"What's going on, Mr. Kim?" said Geoff. Mr. Kim stopped in the corridor and rounded on Geoff. He pointed his finger in Geoff's face, mere inches from his eyeball.

Don't.
Breathe.

Mr. Kim's entire pose was almost exactly the same as his favourite movie poster. Mr. Kim loved movies. He had once confided in Geoff, proudly pointing to himself with his thumb and saying, "Number one gangster." Geoff had smiled politely then and thought of the lads in his manor back home and what they would say. However, today Geoff could see Mr. Kim really believed he was a badass. He jabbed at Geoff's chest -- something that would not have been acceptable back home -- and shouted at the teacher. Geoff could smell the fetid air of his cigarette mouth. He could feel flecks of spittle on his eyelash.

Well, this isn't fun.
Stop.
Breathe.

Geoff would probably never get used to being shouted at in Korean. It wasn't so much the volume or the aggression. It was the fact that he couldn't reply. Not being able to contradict what was being said only seemed to make the other person feel they were in the right and therefore justified in continuing the verbal barrage. Geoff could see a little vein throbbing just under the side parting of his frantic boss. The Englishman put up his hand in peace.

"Mr. Kim, I don't know what you're saying. Why are you angry?"

"Your classroom is a mess! You must clean your classroom after every day!"

Then just say that then.
Don't touch me.
Stop.
Breathe.

16

"I did! I do!" Geoff retorted.

Ish.
Kinda.
Sort of.

The director grabbed Geoff's hand and yanked him towards the classroom. Mr. Kim loved grabbing Geoff and taking him places. The director waved around the room. Geoff looked in cautiously. He had never kept a tidy home but he always tried to keep the workplace clean.

The classroom was as it should be. The desks and chairs were all in place and all the materials were on their shelves. Geoff could not see what the director was talking about at first. Then he noticed the track of paint. It was all purple and formed a meandering line that went all over the ceiling.

Looks nice.
Better than the puke green wallpaper.
Can we just paint the whole thing purple?

"Clean up this mess!" shouted the school director and he stormed off, most likely for another moody cigarette to be smoked in a Hollywood fashion.

How?

He had no soap or mop or anything like that. Mr. Kim was far too cheap to spend money on such luxuries as cleaning tools. Cleaning the classroom generally consisted of using an old brush and pan, dusting ineffectually. The walls were once bright if a terrible choice in colour. Wear and tear showed cracks in the skirting board and countless crayon marks from bored unattended kids over the years.

Geoff touched the purple line of paint. It wasn't strictly a line of paint but rather evenly spaced blotches.

Animal tracks.

Of course that could not be the case. Geoff had never seen tracks like these before. They were tiny, like a bird's but the actual shape was more like a cat's paw.

Besides, what animal can walk upside down?

Geoff traced the line along the ceiling to the wall, moving closely along it. He noticed something that Mr. Kim could not, due to his height. The tracks did not stop on the wall. They carried on to the top shelf and went along it, weaving in and out of the toys gathering dust on display. They were masked from casual view by the books facing out, which made an effective corridor. He walked along the classroom, looking over these books and at the track.

There, about six inches from the end of the shelf the tracks stopped. Curiously they ended in the middle of a print. Geoff stared at it for a while from a distance of about six feet. Something seemed very odd about this last track. He reached out his hand cautiously to touch it.

Suddenly the bell rang. Geoff's classroom was filled with six year olds. He sighed and turned back to his desk. The paint problem would have to wait. He had teaching to do.

Geoff had first thought he would never be a good teacher but he was surprised to find he had an affinity for it. He enjoyed spending time with the kids and his easygoing demeanour made him a favourite with the kids as well. Once he had worked out his rhythm the past two months had gone easily. Geoff tried not to think about the possibility he was just treading water, or that his existence in Korea was tantamount to a familial exile. The life of a schoolteacher in Korea was simple and stress free. He was grateful for that pleasure.

The day unfolded with predictable ease. Class after class, teaching phonics, or focusing on banal conversational skills. The occasional student would be entertaining; the occasional class would be torrid. Geoff let it wash over him as he went into autopilot. This allowed his mind to wander. His eyes flickered upwards and settled on the purple track. His gaze followed the tracks from the back of the classroom and up to the ceiling. Tracing the prints in the opposite direction he had followed them in the morning gave him the impression he was discovering the origin of the tracks rather than the ending. He followed them as they weaved in and out of each other. The tracks went around the ceiling lamp fixture repeatedly. Geoff noticed something new about the tracks as they went around the light. They turned slightly so they were facing towards the light. Then the tracks kept going towards him. He craned his neck upward subtly, hoping his students would not notice his focus of attention. The track stopped right above his head. Geoff stared at it. He looked forward at his students, who were still talking to each other, following the instructions and repeating the same four sentences to each other.

He thought to himself and looked down. There, at his feet were more footprints. They moved under the desk. Geoff swallowed hard and gripped the desk tightly. He closed his eyes for a moment, and then slowly looked under the desk. There was nothing there. The paint tracks went along the floor. These tracks had not been there when he had entered the room with Mr. Kim. These were fresh. Geoff stood up quickly, enough to come to the attention of a few of his more alert students. He ignored them and followed the tracks. They had zigzagged desks and where students had put their feet on the floor. It went back to the paint shelf and then stopped. Geoff looked up but there was no paint to follow.

What was going on?

The last class came and went. Geoff waved everyone good bye, his fixed smile a necessary evil in a job where private education existed in a competitive market. Korean education consisted of half public education, half private education. Parents spent as much on their children's education as the government did. Part of that was an industry of English academies, offering various forms of linguistic development. Most of them were nothing more than babysitters for children whose parents did not want their children to have fun. Some academies wanted to educate but really their primary goal was retaining students and their precious monthly cheque said. Hence, the Academy system was bent towards the parents' desires. Toadying up to parents was far more important to some academies than actually improving children's educations.

Any way you want it.

19

As the last child left Geoff picked up his dust pan and brush and started cleaning. He had no idea what to do about the paint so he decided to leave it until either Mr. Kim or the almost always absent Mrs. Kim did something about it. He had learned that if someone complained about something for long enough, they would take the hint and sort it out by themselves.

Instead, he performed his usual chores in the usual manner. As ever, he started at the back and worked his way to the door. About mid-way, Geoff found himself crouched under the tables and chairs of the second row. Suddenly he heard the sound of books falling to the floor. He got up sharply and hit his head on a chair. Swearing quietly, he put his hand on his head and looked about. There at the back of the classroom some books had fallen off the shelf. He grunted and picked them up.

The wind must have knocked them down.
Only, all the windows are shut.

He walked slowly down the aisle, aware he was alone.

At least, with no one else around.

He reached down and picked up the books. As he was about to put them back with the other books, he noticed something that was not there earlier that morning. An almost empty bottle of purple poster paint was on its side. It must have been hidden from sight by the now fallen books. A drip of paint was threatening to leave its nozzle. The books were also slick with paint on one side.

This side would have been up.

He slowly put the books back, forcing himself to complete the wooden action. His heart hammered wildly and he swallowed nervously. He knew better than to look around the room. He had seen too many scary films to make that mistake. He slowly turned towards the door, and then ran as fast as he could. He reached the classroom door in a second and turned around to turn off the light.

As the lights went off, he was quite sure he saw something move. It was

20

not much. It was bright and blue, like an exposed wire sparking. He saw something else lit up by that moment of electrical luminescence.

He saw enough to make sure he would not turn the light back on.

He shut the door carefully. He walked to the office and picked up his bag. He said goodbye to the other teachers and wondered if he was going to have to keep swallowing. By the time Geoff left the building he could no longer hold it in. He held on to a wall and threw up alongside it.

I need a drink.

3
DOKAEBBI

Geoff walked into In My Memory and nodded to the other foreigners dotted around the pub. This was the extent of his socialising. He bought a beer and sat down at an empty table. Someone had left behind a pad and pencil on the wooden table. He looked around to see if anyone was claiming the bright pink notepad, replete with a bear saying 'Having a morning glory day', but it appeared the morning glory was all for himself. He picked up the pencil and began to doodle as he drank his beer. His doodles started off as typical abstract grids, lines within lines forming spirals and geometric shapes. He found it soothing and let his mind wander. After half an hour, the bar had filled up and the sound of relaxation was annoying him, so he waved over the bar owner and ordered a pitcher of beer. As the beer went down, so did his awareness of others and his drawing became more focused.

He started to draw what he was seeing every time he closed his eyes. What he saw in that classroom became somehow more defined with the alcohol. The yellow fireball eyes glowed more brightly, the mouth showed ever more razor sharp teeth, the blue fur shaggier. The picture took on more definition. Geoff found himself drawing with his head closer and closer to the pad, until at last it was resting sideways. Part of him found the drawing cathartic. In fact, the alcohol in him made him start to consider a career in drawing. He was really quite proud of the picture.

"Excuse me, but I think that's my pad." The voice made Geoff jump for the second time that day. This time, alcohol had a further role to play as the sudden motion made him lose his balance and he fell off his chair. The other ex-pats at the surrounding tables took a break from their insular lives to notice Geoff, to point and giggle or gasp, to judge him on his alcohol intake. The laughter from the surrounding tables was galling enough to make Geoff scramble back up into his chair. He gripped its sides for a second and breathed out noisily. He may have been a little tipsy. He squinted up at the offending voice.

"Sorry! Sorry! Are you okay, man?" American. Geoff could handle the Americans in South Korea. They always seemed so nice, so apologetic about their country. Whilst he had not made friends with them, they seemed to breeze through that friendship making stage and moved right on to discussing their personal lives. Since they never really enquired about his, Geoff let them be. Eventually, everyone would leave him alone so there had not been any long lasting contact. He looked again at the contrite voice and focused. He did not recognise the woman but that was hardly surprising. Despite there being such low numbers of foreigners in the city, Daegu maintained a constant cycle of teachers. In addition to the merry-go-round of fresh faces, there were also those who did not socialise, who only occasionally popped their heads out. She seemed harmless enough. A short, slightly plump body, long black hair and freckles with an upturned nose.

"Yes, Yes, I'm fine. Sorry, sorry about your pad." Geoff slowly scrambled around the table to collect his stuff, making ready to vacate the table. A hand pushed down on his shoulder.

"No Problem. What you drawing there?" With the question, the American sat down and settled into the table. Geoff stared at her for a moment. She did not notice his quizzical look as she held the pad closer to the light

"This is pretty good, uh-"

"...Geoff."

"Geoff. I'm Anne. You draw much better than me." Geoff smiled at that.

"Thanks. I don't normally draw."

"Well, this is a pretty good Dokaebbi."

What?

Anne leaned back to order another pitcher, calling to the bar easily in Korean. When she finished her order and turned back she finally looked at Geoff, who was staring at her. She gave a short self-conscious laugh and brushed her fringe away from her face. "Um, hi there." Geoff realised he must have been staring.

Women.
Ruse.
Fool.

"Dokaebbi? What's that?"

"Dude, you know." She indicated the pad. "I mean you drew a pretty good one. Needs a horn on its forehead but sure, that's a Korean goblin."

"Korean Goblin. Is that an animal?"

Anne started to laugh.

"They're real? I mean they are a real thing?"

"Um, no. They're fantasy. The clue I think is in the name. Goblin. As in goblins and ghouls, goblins and orcs, elves and dwarves, unicorns and dragons..."

"So Dokaebbi are not a real thing." Geoff stared off into the distance. Her laughter had reddened his cheeks. Anne seemed to notice this and she looked apologetically at him.

"How much have you had to drink?"
Geoff looked at Anne intently. He realised he had to stop staring at her

before she freaked out but there was a lot to process.

"Anne, I don't know you at all. But I need to tell someone. I need to get this off my chest. Can you just let me talk at you for a little bit and then-"

"You're kinda freaking me out-"
Geoff slammed the table with his hand. The noise had people looking at them curiously. Anne did not move for a second. She then turned her head sideways at him.

"If you want my help, do not ever do something like that again." Her voice had a warning tone, with the addition of the confidence of being able to back it up. Geoff put his hands up for a moment, and then slowly put them into the center of the table before sliding them back along the table to his lap. The lacquer against his skin was calming.

He spoke softly and slowly. "I do not mean to freak you out. I am freaked out and I do not know anyone else here. I've lived in this country for three months and have not made one friend, one person with whom I can talk. Can I just talk?"

They looked at each other. Anne smiled and took his hand in hers.

"We all need a friend sometime. Shoot."
Geoff looked at her soft smiling face and breathed. He spoke for a while, telling her everything that had happened during the day. The pitcher of beer came and went, Anne pouring for the both of them. She did not interrupt once and she listened in such a way that Geoff did not doubt her attention at any point. At last he finished. She nodded to herself and emptied her glass. She stood up.

"Come on. Let's go."

"Go? Go where?"

"To your *hagwan*, silly. Let's go find your goblin."

4
TORCHED

Geoff and Anne stepped out of the bar into the night. Daegu was ringed by mountains so the weather when hot during the day tended to retain its heat at night. During the rare mild parts of the year, this made for very pleasant evenings. Daegu with over two million inhabitants. Grid road systems were new to Geoff, as were roads with literally no names. At night, red electric crosses shone from the tops of myriad churches. Geoff had been surprised to find so many Christians in this part of the world. Sometimes, when he looked beyond the city limits, he would remind himself to take a hike in the mountains but Sunday mornings seemed to be better spent in bed.

The carbon copy white towers of the neighborhood apartments dwarfed Geoff and Anne. As they walked down the street, avoiding the random bits of debris that littered the kerb, they chatted amiably about life in Korea. Geoff found that Anne had lived in the country for over seven years, and that she pretty much knew all that was happening in the expat community. Geoff was surprised there was anything like a community; he had not seen any evidence of that. Then again, he only went to the same bar and never went downtown. Avoiding people had seemed necessary. Anne was of the opposite opinion. She believed knowing people was essential to surviving long term in a foreign country. Geoff did not have the heart to dissuade her of that fanciful notion.

The school building was unlike most of the others on the main drag. It was filled with darkness. Daegu was a mass of neon and fairy lights. Business men would drink soju on weekdays until the early morning hours. As the two teachers watched and smiled to themselves, one old *ajoshi* was carried to a taxi by his younger underlings. One couple walked past them, the man holding onto the woman's forearm loosely but definitively as he led her down the street. Geoff glowered at that and stopped. He had been raised to never mistreat women. Leading her like she was a dog on a leash rankled deeply. He looked on at them for a while as Anne checked the door.

After a moment or two she turned triumphantly to Geoff.

"They didn't lock the door!"

"Really? They usually do." Geoff was surprised. Anne shrugged her shoulders and opened the door.

"Guess they forgot. Let's take the stairs. I don't want anyone to hear us using the lift." With that she moved up the stairwell. Despite her size, she moved with both alacrity and silence. Geoff shook his head in surprise. Anne was proving to have many hidden qualities. He joined her. He prided himself on never using the lift anyway. People who could not go up nine flights of stairs needed to question their living habits. When they got to the top, Geoff held Anne back. She looked at him in annoyance.

"What?"

"You don't know the layout. Let me go first and make sure Mr. Kim is not working late."

Anne looked like she was going to retort but bit down, thinking better of it. Geoff crept past her and tried the entrance. The glass door slid open noiselessly. Geoff could hear a mumbling of sorts coming from Mr. Kim's office. He bear crawled to the side of the office door which was only slightly ajar. He looked through and his eyes widened at the spectacle unfolding.

27

He motioned for Anne to follow him. She joined him next to the office and Geoff pointed to the end of the corridor. Anne stayed crouched down and moved down the corridor. Geoff joined her. They crept up the stairs. At night, the stairs and corridor to Geoff's classroom looked even more foreboding. Anne pulled out a torch from her backpack.

"So, is Mr. Kim working?" whispered Anne. Geoff hesitated to find the right words before answering.

"He's uh, He's watching the game on telly. He's not alone. He is also with Miss Huang." He looked pointedly at Anne. She opened her mouth in understanding, then smothered a giggle.

"Well, at least when he tells his wife he was watching the game, he wasn't lying."

"Why do you have a torch with you?"

"Torch, you English are so funny. I hear torch, I think those things you see on fire on beaches." She felt for Geoff's class room door handle and turned it. The door opened and Anne went in.

"Oh, so I suppose flashlight is better. It's not. It's not a flash of light; it's a constant stream of light." Anne turned and looked at Geoff. She slowly put her finger to her lips and looked pointedly at him. Geoff put up his hands defensively. She turned around and started following the footprints around the room. Geoff walked slowly over to his desk and leaned against it, watching the American looking around.

It's like she's hunting prey.

He noticed she kept one hand in her backpack, the other clasped around the torch. Her face would bend low to where the spots of paints were, until her nose was only inches away from them. As Geoff watched with interest, she plucked a hair off the ground. She carefully put it into a test tube and corked it.

"Just .... carry around test tubes, do ya??" whispered Geoff sarcastically. Anne looked at him sheepishly.

"Okay, look, I just really like animals." She had the decency to look sheepish as Geoff glowered at her.

"Okay, fine. We had a science class today and I swiped them from the kits for the kids. I was going to do some soju shots. Are you happy now?" Geoff relented, breaking out into a wide grin. She grinned back. Then she spun her head towards the back of the room. "Did you see that?"

Geoff had seen that. Out of the corner of his eye, a sudden flash of blue. As he turned to face it, Anne's flashlight cut across his eye line for a moment and he was blinded. As his vision recovered, the beam of light was splayed against the back of the wall. Here were pictures that the children had drawn of different geometric shapes. They had labelled them, indicating their colour and shape. An orange square, a red rectangle. A blue circle. Anne flashed it for a moment then grunted, moving on.

Geoff ignored her movements and proceeded slowly to the bookshelf. His footsteps were slow and deliberate and attracted Anne's attention. She stopped looking at the back of the room. She came close to Geoff and together they stood in front of the bookshelf. As Geoff reached out for the first display book, his hand trembled. Just as he touched, a low guttural sound filled the empty room. It was a menacing growl.

The growl did not come from the bookshelf. It came from above them. Slowly, the two teachers looked up. Anne kept her torch facing down. Geoff yelled and ran for the door. He heard Anne's footsteps behind him. He reached the door and jerked it open as Anne tumbled through. Holding it open, he studied the room. He saw no sign of the creature. In fact, the last thing he saw was the blue circle on the wall. It glistened and shimmered.

What was that?

Geoff did not have time to think. Anne had stumbled out into the corridor and Geoff ran after her. Her feet got caught up in themselves and Geoff ran full pelt into her. They tumbled and landed heavily against Mr. Kim's office door. It swung open and everyone saw everyone.

29

5
CONFRONATION

The scene was a frozen tableau. Mr. Kim and Miss Huang were in a position that Mrs. Kim would not have appreciated at all. Geoff had wondered why Mr. Kim had kept the children's *papier mache* balloon heads on his desk. Now he was just thankful they blocked the full scene. It was probably unfortunate that it was a pair of laughing clown faces that provided most of the discretion.

Anne had not moved since her hand covered her mouth and her eyes were now just goggling. Geoff thought she had been fighting the urge to scream but she was visibly shaking from her attempt to not burst out laughing. Meanwhile, the Englishman had maintained his composure. He stared and his mouth was slightly open but otherwise his composure was fine.

The split second of shame stretched into infinity then snapped back into reality. Miss Huang's eyes widened, and then she screamed, bolting off behind the supply cupboard at the back of the office. Geoff could still see her feet sticking out, her painted nails quaking. Mr. Kim stared at Anne and Geoff, who could only stare back in the situation presented. To look anywhere else would have led to indelibly burned images. Mr. Kim's face ran through a gamut of emotions, starting with anger, then

30

fear, then and only then, and only for a moment, embarrassment, before returning inevitably to anger.

"Get out! Now!" He shouted. Geoff and Anne had to shake their heads out of their awful reverie. Geoff motioned at Anne to go. She stumbled out of the office, nodding thankfully at Geoff, and practically ran out of the main door. Geoff looked at the swinging glass door and wondered if he should go as well.

If I leave now I am saying this is my fault and I get fired.
Bugger that.

Geoff stretched his neck and rolled it from side to side. This was one of his favoured methods of getting psyched for a battle. His neck cracked; it had been a long time since Geoff had gotten psyched for a battle.

Been a long time since I've been psyched about anything.

He looked at Mr. Kim and grimaced.

Miss Huang screamed again.

"*Hajima!*" Geoff said, injecting as much ice into the command, to stop, as he dared. He would never have adopted this tactic in England. However, based upon his experiences of how the Koreans spoke to one another, asserting control seemed akin to brinkmanship mixed with good old fashioned sexism. The young lady began to quiet down and reduced her sobs to a more ladylike level. Mr. Kim opened his mouth to speak.

"Mr. Kim, put on your pants and come to my classroom please. Miss Huang, you shall wait here." With that, Geoff spun on his heel and walked to his classroom.

Where the monster is.

Geoff's pace slowed; he had no desire to face those teeth again. However, he had set the location and could not change it. He stamped with each step and whistled loudly. He had heard people would do this in the wild, to scare away small, dangerous creatures.

31

Which assumes the creature knows what fear is.

As he got to the classroom, he reached in quickly and turned on the lights. He walked in, steeling himself. He looked around, starting with the ceiling right by the door. The classroom was empty but Geoff was not fooled.

"If there are any monsters in here, I need you to stay the hell out of my way. Do you understand?" whispered Geoff to the empty rows of chairs. He put on his best teacher voice. "I said, D?"

"Understand what?" Geoff spun round to see Mr. Kim walk over to a chair. He was still stuffing his shirt into his trousers. Geoff had called them pants because he knew the Koreans used American English. The teacher leaned against his table, a model of nonchalance, and looked down at his boss. He took a deep breath and adopted the tone Mr. Kim usually reserved for his teachers that had failed him in some way. As a recipient of this tone on a regular occasion, Geoff was intimate with its cadence.

"Do you understand…do you understand….how embarrassing this is for me? How embarrassing this is for Miss Huang? How embarrassing this is for your wife?"

"I don't think you understand what was happen-"

"Don't you dare say I didn't see you doing what you and I both know full well what you were doing." Both men paused as they thought over this sentence, making sure it made sense. They both grunted to themselves. "Don't call me a liar. Ever!"

"I, well, I…." Geoff let Mr. Kim sputter on for a moment. He ran out of steam and sat down miserably in one of the student seats. The tall teacher pushed himself off the desk. He loomed over the boss in his elementary schoolchild's seat. He spoke thoughtfully.

"Maybe I could forget this happened. Maybe it would be better for everyone involved if you and I had never been here tonight. What do you think?"

"Tell her, no one could possibly believe you over me." Mr. Kim said. Geoff recognised this tone as well. False bravado poured off the Korean like cheap aftershave.

Although that could admittedly be the cheap aftershave he uses.

"Sure, let's find out if you like. I guess I will see you in the morning and I'll talk to her then." Geoff turned to go out of the classroom.

Was that a small flash of blue by the cupboard?

"No!" the cry shot out of Mr. Kim, and he looked the most surprised about it. Geoff walked to the back of the classroom. He looked at the cupboard. He spoke without looking at his boss, the man who ostensibly controlled his job security.

"In the meantime, I have to clean up this classroom and you can either help me, call the police and have me thrown out, or go home and pretend we never saw each other. It really is none of my concern." Geoff was amazed how he was able to channel his inner Snob when threatened. It really spoke to his mother's upbringing. Mr. Kim got up, a disheveled, dismal, showing of a man. He walked slowly to the doorway, and then paused.

"I expect to see you tomorrow at work, Geoff."

Geoff turned his head to the paint pots and looked levelly at the blue creature staring right back at him. The creature made no sound and stood perfectly still. Its fur bristled ever so slightly as if being hit by wind. The Englishman nodded almost imperceptibly and smiled a little smile.

"I expect so. Good night, sir. I have work to do."

Mr. Kim walked out of the classroom and Geoff cared not at all. His job seemed secure and he cared not at all. He had won a personal life battle, unaided, for the first time in what seemed like forever, and he cared not at all. He looked at the creature. It was baring its teeth.

No, no it's not. It's smiling.

6
CONTACT

He stared at the creature. It stood up on two legs and it was clear that it was bipedal. Its feet were paws, shaped like a bear, with three short sharp claws raised above the surface of the bookshelf. Its hands were by contrast delicate, elongated, with its colour blue being extended to its skin, and not just its lustrous fur. In the light of the classroom, it was a delight, starting a light sky blue at its base, darkening to a charcoal grey as it climbed up its back, cresting into a passable imitation of a mane as it met the creature's shoulders. The creature's eyes were as wide as a bush baby's. Its large black pupils clearly showed Geoff's reflection. However, instead of that creature's skinny frail arms, this animal had robust musculature.

Yes, robust. That was the word. This animal could survive where others could not.

If its hands were out of proportion, then its ears were surely plain outsized. They pushed through the dark mane stretching out and were constantly moving slowly, snaking around at the slightest sound in the vicinity.

It moves quicker than anything you've ever seen before. It can hide better than almost anything and has the ability to hear things you can't.

35

It cocked its head, its ears flapping slowly down until their tips touched its rounded chin. It opened its mouth as if to speak, then pursed its lips and looked inscrutably at Geoff.

It wanted to be found by you.

Geoff raised a hand up. "Hello," he said slowly.

The creature raised its hand up, mirroring Geoff. Then, it leapt up and high fived him. He landed on the shelf and gesticulated at the teacher. As he fought to control his heart hammering at his chest, Geoff stared at the creature.

So fast. He could have clawed my eyes out.

It was pointing its index fingers at him and had both of its thumbs up. Geoff stared at the creature.

"Are... are you doing finger guns?" Geoff frequently used high fives and finger guns in the classroom. His students loved them. Had this creature been watching him for longer than he realised?

You thought of him as 'he' just then. You're still thinking that way.

The thought ran through his brain and he lowered his head to the same level as the....

What? As the what?

"What do I call you? I'm Geoff." He said to the creature. He prodded his chest with his thumb, Tarzan style. "Geoff. Day-Veeed."

The creature slowly drifted forward, small steps carrying him to the edge of the shelf. He opened his mouth, then slowly shook his head. He pointed to his throat then shook his head. Slowly, he held out his hand and placed it palm side against Geoff's unresisting cheek. It was surprisingly raspy and Geoff could feel the tiny claws at the tips of the fingers. The teacher slowly brought his fingers up to touch the paw.

36

The creature's eyes misted and Geoff's reflection shimmered then disappeared. Geoff found himself staring into those pools. The pools shifted, then began to whirl, slowly at first, then sped up. Geoff started to panic.

Do not be afraid.

The thought only might have been Geoff's. Images flew through him in a violent nonsensical blur. At one point a laughing shadow. Another, a tower. Another, a bird being violently ripped apart.

Geoff blinked his eyes and shook his head. As he did so, something snapped in his mind and he felt his soul float free. He stared hard at the creature. The creature's eyes had shined. Then, those eyes closed. When they reopened, they had resumed their original frame. Geoff's reflection started within them. If it was possible, the creature looked disappointedly at Geoff.

"What? What's wrong?" murmured Geoff.

The creature turned away and suddenly ran towards the back of the classroom. Geoff reached out for him but the blue creature was already moving. When the bookshelf ended he leaped powerfully into the air. As it seemed as if he must surely slam against the wall, he disappeared.

Geoff's jaw dropped. There, right in the wall, set into the blue circle poster, a shimmer of light crackled. It parted a tad, forming an ever so slightly larger circle. Now, a reddish hue of light shone through. Geoff moved slowly to it. He approached it from the side, grimly accepting of this chosen path. His head leaned against the wall. From this side, nothing could be seen. The light did not pour out like a beam of light should. Geoff thought on that for a moment.

If I cannot see the light from here, how am I able to see it from over there?

His understanding of physics was not good, but he understood that much.

It must be magic.

37

Sarcastic thoughts aside, Geoff could not explain what he was seeing. He moved himself so he was standing right in front of the shimmering red spot. Geoff could not quite understand why, but he felt like he had just failed an important test. He stared into the hole for a long time but nothing and no one came out.

What are you?

7
LESSONS

The next day passed without anything of note. Mr. Kim stayed in his office the entire time Geoff was in the school. Miss Huang was mysteriously very busy with paperwork whenever Geoff was in the same room. He was thankful for the lack of discussion. Any attempt at hand wringing, or self-justification, or moralistic self-flagellation, whilst cathartic for the Koreans would have been most unpleasant to the young man.

Furthermore, being left alone could afford him the opportunity to rendezvous with the creature. Unfortunately, it was not to be. Throughout the day, and the day after, and the days that followed, there was no sign of the blue furry creature.

Geoff reset his classroom, angling the tables and chairs so that he had line of sight to the circle poster at the back of the room. It had changed colour again. Now it was black. It occurred to the teacher on the third day this meant anyone looking from the other side may then be able to see him just as well. After a week, his eyes were suffering from the strain of staring at the space by the paint pots. When his students wore anything with powder blue, he would see a flash of their clothing out of the corner of his eye. Whirling around he would stare at the unfortunate student who had dare wear a blue cap or tshirt and silently curse the

39

creature's lack of interest.

Every night since she had seen Mr. Kim and Miss Huang, Anne had greeted Geoff outside his school building. She always started the conversation off with "So?" and would continue to probe Geoff for any new information. Geoff had told her everything about the creature. His drawings became inspired; he had never drawn this well. When drawing the creature, it was as if his hand was guided. He had not told Anne about the circle. It still seemed impossible to himself, let alone sensible enough to explain to someone else.

It was one week later when Geoff came out of the building rubbing his eyes, feeling the beginnings of a strain headache coming on. He looked around and noticed Anne was not waiting for him. He felt his phone vibrate as a text was delivered. It was from Anne.

Come to In My Memory. I have an idea about Blue.

Blue is absolutely the perfect name for him.

Geoff set off for In My Memory at a regular pace, the sun setting over the mountains in front of him. By the time Geoff entered the dimly lit tavern, Anne was already ensconced at a booth in a corner. Her table held a stack of papers. Geoff waved to her and went to the bar. He needed a beer after the week he had gone through. Taking a deep draught, he then took the glass over to Anne's table and sat down heavily, sighing. Anne either ignored or didn't notice his dramatic entrance.

"So, I think you have been coming at this the wrong way." She took a sip from her pint and reached for a piece of paper in the pile.

"I don't know what you mean. What are all these?"

"Well, you have been looking and waiting and watching. Right?"

"Right."

"Those are pretty reactive actions. I think you need to be proactive. It's time you go get him."

"Go get him? Where do you think he is?"

She knows. Of course she knows.

"What do you want me to do, smoke him out, reach in with a hook?"

Anne smiled at him and put down the paper. She leaned forward conspiratorially. "Sorta. Look, I think he wanted to communicate with you. He wanted to talk to you."

"How, telepathy?"

"Telepathy might be right." Anne smiled at him, leaning out of her conspiratorial mood. Blue had made her quite excited. She had come up with ten other such ideas in the last week. The tavern had done quite well from their meetings in the last seven days.

Geoff snorted. "Oh come on!"

"What? Do you have any idea about this thing? About where's it's from? About anything?"

"Okay, let's pretend it is telepathic. How does that help me, since I am not?"

"It doesn't, except that makes him open to dialogue. You can communicate with it, if you follow this plan." With that, Anne pulled out of the pile a single sheet. Geoff glanced at it for a second. It was a lesson plan. It was, in fact, a perfect lesson plan. Geoff had learned on the job from a template the Korean management had given him. He had also seen examples on the Internet. However, this was by far the most well-ordered, edited and succinct lesson plan he had seen.

"You want me to...teach it English?"

"Why not? You already do phonics in your classroom."

How do you know that?

41

"Just start again from the beginning. Focus on these lessons in particular and you have enough to find out if it can understand the basics."

"And what makes you think he is even paying attention?" Geoff slumped back in his chair and took a swig. "This bloody thing just pops in my life then runs off."

Anne laughed. "I love it when English people swear. You sound so proper." Geoff smiled at her. In the last ten days, their friendship had blossomed. She was always so upbeat and entertained by him, it was impossible not to like her. Also, Geoff had been starved of human interaction.

You do it to yourself, you do.

He raised his glass towards her and she raised hers in return.

"Don't worry" she said, "you're too interesting for this guy to shy away."

Geoff spent the weekend going over Anne's lesson plans. He had never been particularly gifted in this field. Often, his lessons consisted of working from the book and goofing around. Now he found himself nodding along to her set syllabus. While he initially found it daunting, after a while he understood the processes. More than that, he had grown an appreciation of the art of teaching. He had been treading water these past few months. Meanwhile, Anne had shown him in a few pieces of paper the basic building blocks to being a better teacher. By the time Monday morning rolled around he had his game plan and he strolled into the academy, whistling.

"Geoff, no whistling." The command came from the open door of Mr. Kim's office. Geoff stopped and took a step back, allowing him to look into the office. Mr. Kim looked steadily into Geoff's eyes.

"No whistling. Okay?" A moment passed between them.

He needs a win.

"Yes, boss." They both nodded at each other and Geoff walked down the corridor to his classroom. He was glad it appeared like bridges were being rebuilt, albeit in a strangled form.

He had a lot to prepare for his coming day. Firstly, he took the teacher's copy of the class book and placed it at the back of the classroom, right next to a new blue paint pot, placed in the space vacated by the previous pot. He was careful to make sure the book was open to today's lesson. Next to the book, he left his shortest pencil, almost sharpened right up to the eraser tip. Finally, he took a poster of the alphabet and stuck it up on the bookshelf next to the paint pots. On a random whim he took off the lid for the blue paint pot.

Any way you want it.

During all of this, he was painfully aware of his proximity to the circle.

It's not a goddamn circle. Stop reducing things.

He kept his eyes looking downward, careful to make sure he never looked into the black.

Door.
Portal.
Rift.
Any way you want it.

As his students came into the classroom, he greeted them then got on with the new lesson plan. Before he started the workbook, Geoff wrote his name slowly on the board, exaggerating each movement. Then he went through each letter of his name, sounding it out, repeating each sound five times. He then had the whole class repeat it back to him, before asking every student to sound it out individually. Then he had the students say their name, writing their name on the board and then sounding it out in front of their classmates. He thought they would be bored doing this but he was quite surprised. They showed attentive enthusiasm and Geoff was infected by their energy. Before he knew it, the lesson was almost out of time. Somehow they were still able to finish their workbook pages as the bell rang and the kids high fived Geoff as they happily bounced out of the classroom. One child gave Geoff his beloved finger gun salute and Geoff returned it with a smile.

43

Geoff smiled wryly to himself.

Damn me if that wasn't the best lesson I ever had.

He glanced for a moment to the back of the room as a reflex, then remembering his plan of avoidance, looked away again.

The rest of the day followed the same exact lesson plan. Students showed a desire to be a part of the lesson in a way Geoff had never managed before and he wondered how much time he had been wasting. When the last bell had rung and Geoff was alone in the classroom, he cleaned up. Chairs were pushed under tables and scrap paper and pencils left behind were collected. He slowly worked his way to the back of the classroom. He was apprehensive about what he might find there. Finally, Geoff looked at the paint-pot area. The pencil was in the same exact position where he'd left it. The work book was untouched. Geoff sighed to himself. He knew it was a long shot but there had been that feeling at one point that he was really … teaching and now he suddenly felt deflated.

As he picked up the notebook and the pencil, his eyes glanced towards the alphabet poster. He froze. The poster had both uppercase and lowercase letters printed on it. The capital D, along with its lowercase alternate were both imprinted with a single paw print of blue paint. So was the lowercase 'a', 'i' and 'v'.

Geoff looked slowly around the empty room. He took the poster, stuffing it into his satchel and walked out of the academy, already texting Anne to meet him at In My Memory.

Ladies and gentlemen, start your engines.

8
EXPANSION

"Why do you think all movie aliens are blue?" wondered Anne. She supped at her beer.

In Korea, bars would stay open until the last customer left, even if that was at nine in the morning to go right back to work. Drinking was an essential part of the Korean culture. Business deals were transacted, friendships and vendettas refreshed anew over beer and soju.

Around Geoff and Anne were groups of other teachers, and one small table of Korean businessmen who were getting increasingly louder as they drank. Geoff looked at his friend who was propping up her head with her hand, elbow occasionally swaying under the weight. She didn't look drunk but she definitely looked like she'd been drinking.

"What do you mean?" he slurred. "Predator was invisible. Alien alien, the alien from Alien, that was black." He had brought the poster to In My Memory and they had both congratulated each other on the successful contact. Congratulations had turned to toasting each other, and slowly they had wound down to pontification.

"Avatar was blue. Mac and Me, blue..."

45

"He was gray! So was Paul, so were the Independence Day Aliens. They were all gray!"

"They *were* gray! Why did I think all aliens were blue?"

"Avatar. You got Avatar."

"And Blue."

"You think he's an alien?"

"Of course! What did you think?"

I'm just glad you saw it too. Else I'm crazy.

"I don't know. Some kind of … monster?"

"Monster? He's adorable."

"Right now. He could get bigger. And meaner."

"Do you really think so?"

"Sure. Why not? No. Not really. He's fine." Geoff rubbed his temples. "So, I should carry on with the phonics?"

"Sure. Can you wipe the paint off the poster?"

"Let me try." Geoff fished out the poster again from his satchel. He poured some beer on the laminated surface then wiped it off with some paper napkins. The blue paint came off fairly well, although there was a faint outline of the paw-prints left on the poster.

"That'll do," said Geoff and he put the poster back in the satchel without looking. As he stuffed it in there, his hand touched against something furry. He looked in the bag.

Blue looked up at him and smiled. The rows of teeth had seemed to recede. The satellite ears had perked up as Geoff looked at Blue. Geoff smiled broadly, then looked around guiltily. He put his finger to his lips

46

and Blue mimicked him instantly. Geoff smiled again. Blue smiled back. Geoff slowly waved into his bag. Blue waved back.

"What you doing?" slurred Anne.

"Anne, I think we should get out of here. Let's head to the park."

"Come on, man, I got half a beer here."

"Anne, look at me. Look at me, Anne."

Anne looked at him.

"We need to go to the park now."

"Okay." Anne slid out of the booth and grabbed her backpack. She waved goodbye to the other teachers who waved back uninterestedly. They walked out of the bar and headed off to one of the many nearby urban parks.

"So," began Anne, "What is going on? Are you going to make a move on me?"

"What? No!"

"Way to make a lady feel wanted."

"What?"

"Jeez, Geoff, I'm kidding. Calm down."

Women.
Ruse.
Fool.
Shut up.

"Okay."

"So, what's going on?"

"Let's get to the park. I need somewhere private."

They walked through the open entrance of the park. It was a small area, ringed with a low metal fence. Inside, there were the usual array of weird rusty gym equipment the older Koreans seemed to love so much. Daegu was full of these little parks - small closed off fake areas of green serenity. In the centre there was a small pagoda, normally big enough for four people to sit down and have a drink. The two teachers sat down heavily. Geoff carefully put his satchel in the center. Anne looked at him inquisitively.

"He's here, Anne. He's in my satchel." Geoff had sobered up, and his whispered statement had a similar effect on his friend in an instant.

"Blue?"

The satchel shook and flapped open. The moonlight hit Blue, lighting up his fur as he stood up and looked around. His eyes grew very big and he ducked under the bag.

"Hey Blue, wanna come out of there?" Geoff carefully slid the satchel's sides down. Blue looked at Geoff and smiled, before suddenly diving headfirst into Geoff's lap.

Teeth!

Then the head popped out again and looked around. Geoff breathed out again, a little harder than he intended. The first thing Blue focused on was Anne, who was open mouthed. Blue mimicked her slack-jawed expression perfectly. Geoff laughed. Blue looked around, alarmed at the sound.

Who's afraid of laughter?

Blue then turned back to Anne. He smiled at her and waved. Anne's eyes widened and after a moment she cautiously waved back. She slowly crawled over to Blue, keeping her body low to the dirty planking. Her face came within inches of Blue before stopping. She marvelled at his body.

48

"Can I touch him?" she whispered.

"Maybe you should ask him." Anne looked startled at Geoff who shrugged his shoulders at her.

"He spelled my name out. Blue is a him, not an it. You don't ask someone else if it is cool to talk to me, do you?"

Anne looked at Blue and spoke as slowly as when she talked to her pre-starter children.

"Can I …touch…you?" This was punctuated by slow, definite gesticulation, the penultimate word matched with two hands touching and the last word pointing softly at Blue.

Just so good at being a teacher.
He should have found her, not me.

The little creature looked at Geoff who shrugged his shoulders again.

Don't ask me, chap.
I have no idea about her.

Blue held out his arms wide and grabbed hold of Anne's cheeks. He brought her close to him and then kissed her on the lips. Anne giggled.

"Why, sir! You need to take me out for a dinner first!" She put the mildest of admonition in her voice and tapped him lightly on his nose. Blue stepped back in surprise, then wrinkled his nose and smiled full beam at Anne.

"Right, you, let's get you home."

"My house?" asked Geoff.

"No, his house. What do you think, Blue, you wanna go home?"

"His house? I can't keep breaking into my *hagwan*. I don't think I want to see any more of Miss Huang, if you know what I am saying."

49

I hate myself.

"No one does, except maybe Mr. Kim. But Blue can't stay here." Geoff had to agree with Anne. He suddenly thought of his dirty one-room excuse for an apartment. The school had given him an apartment covered with mold on one wall. Whilst he had done his best to clean it, he did not trust his apartment to bring a girl home to it, let alone an alien species.

Blue looked alarmed at Geoff then dove into the satchel.

"What is it, Blue?" said Geoff. He looked around the park. They were alone. A police car slowly went past them, its constant silent flashing lights lighting up the road.

"Don't worry chap, it's just the police," laughed Geoff. Blue did not come out of the satchel. Geoff shrugged. He could understand why someone would be scared of weird flashing lights moving along. "Alright then, let's take you home. Anne, you're coming along, I assume?" She nodded sweetly, smiling so brightly her eyes were shut.

The two of them walked down the street to the main road where the majority of the *hagwans* were collected. The bright lights of a city that never really sleeps illuminated their progress, allowing them to dodge the giant mounds of rubbish bags left out every night. The smell of raw sewage lessened at night but it was still powerful enough on occasion to make Geoff's nose twitch and Anne to gag. The number of people on the streets at night in the suburban area where they lived was quite low but there was a steady stream of traffic flying past. They walked past the more successful *hagwans* and arrived at the tower where the Geoff's *hagwan* was housed.

"Uh, let me see if the door is locked again."

How can she break in so well?

"Anne, mate, I'm not stupid. You're breaking in. I don't mind, just don't lie to me."

A moment of silence between them, then Anne nodded.

50

What else you lied to me about?
Woman.
Ruse.
Shut up.
She's your only friend.
Apart from Blue.

Geoff and Anne got in the glass elevator and they went up to the top floor. The *hagwan* was not locked again. As they came in, Geoff and Anne could hear the all too familiar grunts and moans.

"I can't believe it. They're at it again!" whispered Geoff fiercely.

"Well, she is certainly agreeing with him a lot. Shall we leave them to it?" suggested Anne.

"Hang on a minute. Miss Huang doesn't speak English that well. I don't think she knows that particular idiom." Geoff crept to the side of the Director's office door and looked in cautiously. He stared for a moment and then crept back to Anne.

"Well, the good news is Miss Huang is not involved. The bad news is, Mr. Kim may well be going blind soon. Come on." They crept past the office, the television glare illuminating Mr. Kim's intensely focused stare.

They went into Geoff's classroom and Geoff reached for the classroom light. He stopped when Anne grabbed him and pointed urgently at the back of the classroom.

They stared mutely at the scene.

The room was filled with dappled sunlight and the sound of birds chirping at each other. One quarter of the classroom back wall was obscured by the view of a gnarled old tree covered in red leaves. Just beyond it the glimpse of a purple sky and rolling brown hills suggested at much, much more.

"It's gotten bigger," breathed Anne. She approached it softly. Geoff stared hard at the back of her head, jaw clenched in anger.

I never told you about the rift.

"I am definitely getting fired," said Geoff. His satchel flap opened and Blue looked up at Geoff. He raised his eyebrows in acknowledgement then clambered easily out of the bag. He ran nimbly, then jumped onto a desk, before launching himself into the portal and onto one of the tree limbs. When he got to the trunk, he turned and waved at the teachers who could only mutely wave back. Then, Blue disappeared from view.

"We better get to work," said Anne, putting down her back pack.

"What do you mean?" said Geoff.

"We need to hide this from your kids and your coworkers by seven. I think that gives you maybe six hours. That's more than enough time to hide this."

"Hide this? Hide this?" He walked up to the sunny vista, edged by the ever present electric blue shimmer. "How the hell do we hide this?" He motioned wildly and he felt his hand go into the portal. For a brief moment he felt the wind of another planet, felt the heat of another sun. His hand stayed where it was and he flexed his fingers there.

I could crawl through there if I wanted to.

I wonder how long until I could walk through.

How big is this going to get?

9
INSPECTION

Geoff woke up under his classroom table and groaned. His back was killing him and he had pins and needles in his arms. As he half-crawled, half-shuffled out from under the cramped space, he groaned loudly. He stretched and forced himself up into a standing position. He stared blearily at his phone's face. He had about four hours sleep which was impressive considering the amount of work they had done last night. Anne had said her goodbyes and gone home. He envied her work schedule allowing her the mornings off but had been grateful for her vital help.

He stretched again, feeling his back bones crackle and stared at the night's work. A huge black cloth had been found at the bottom of his room's supply closet. It was erected across the length of the entire classroom. It was about a yard before the wall, concealing the portal and the back shelves filled with books neither Geoff nor any other teacher had ever used. On the cloth were pinned posters of the alphabet and the body, along with selected pictures the children had drawn and that, luckily as it turned out, Geoff had hoarded in his desk drawer. Finally, the tables and chairs had been brought closer together. Geoff hoped the children would not notice how much of the classroom had been lost behind the cloth. He also hoped he would not fall asleep in any of his lessons.

He walked out of the classroom and washed his face in the bathroom. As he came out, he saw Mr. Kim. The man looked the worse for wear. Geoff had not heard the director leave the office. He knew Mr. Kim kept a roll up bed behind his desk, for those occasions where he would have a solo soju drinking session and sleep it off away from the wrath of Mrs. Kim.

"You're here early, Geoff. That's good. How are you?" The man looked quite cheery this morning for a man suffering from a dreaded soju hangover.

"Oh, I am feeling great. Time to do some teaching!" Geoff was quite surprised at how well he could toady up to authority sometimes. The director went into his office, probably not to be seen for the rest of the day and Geoff went back to his classroom to prepare for his day.

The first lesson went well and the children left happily even though there were some noticeable issues. The biggest problem was the noise. Birds chirped almost constantly. At one point, there was a distant but disturbing lowing sound. Geoff was quite sure he was going to be found out, but the kids seemed to enjoy the ambient sound. Mrs. Kim came in during one of the five minute breaks and nodded approvingly at the new décor. She put a hand to her ear as she heard the bird sounds.

"CD," said Geoff and she laughed delightedly, clapping her hands together.

"Very good, Geoff. You are doing a good job!" Geoff shook his head and smiled as she walked out of the classroom.

When the kindergarteners left at lunchtime, Geoff had an opportunity to inspect the back of the cloth. There was a bright shaft of moonlight coming through the branches of the tree. It illuminated the scene quite well but there were no signs of life. Geoff was quite happy about that. The deep lowing sound had frankly terrified Geoff. It had put him in mind of a lion or a bear or something else that was big and hungry. However, he was a little sad he couldn't see Blue anywhere. He hoped the little guy was okay. During a break, he called for him through the cloth in an urgent manner but he refrained from calling loudly. There was no response, so Geoff left his teacher's book and alphabet poster next to an open paint pot behind the curtain. He was very careful to not look at the portal.

The elementary school students came in the afternoon and the lessons continued. It was during the penultimate lesson that Geoff noticed the blanket was moving. Something was bumping against the back of the blanket, making the posters and pictures wobble about. The children were singing along with a CD as this happened, so only Geoff was facing the makeshift wall. He sang loudly with the children and anxiously watched the wall's movements.

E-I-E-I- O nonono!

There was a loud squawk and the wall stopped billowing. The squawk turned a few of the students' heads but when there was no follow up sound they turned around again. After that brief moment, the day's lessons ended without further drama. When the students were all gone, Geoff cleaned the room. He checked to make sure none of the other teachers were coming towards his classroom, then made his way to the curtain. He opened it up and finally looked at the rift. It was now much lighter, clearly it was now coming to its sunrise. On the floor of the classroom there was a dead bird. Geoff could tell it was dead because its neck was at an unnatural angle. Some red feathers had come loose from its tail. Next to them was the alphabet poster. There were fresh paw prints. They were over the lower case letters "b" "d' "i" and "r".

Someone's building their vocabulary.

He stepped into the space behind the curtain. He knew he would be left alone in his classroom for at least an hour. Most teachers would be at their desks, prepping for the next day. Mr. Kim would be either sleeping it off, or doing Mrs. Kim's bidding. He put his hands on his hips and surveyed the panorama on display. He angled his head round but could not quite see around the tree.

A whole world in front of me and someone put a bloody tree in front of my view.

Oh well, why not?

He took a deep breath and poked his head through. Instantly the wind blew his hair back. It was much cooler than in the sweltering summer of Daegu.

In for a penny.

He breathed out. Closing his eyes tight, he took a deep breath. The air tasted dry but fresh. He opened his eyes and laughed. "I am officially a space explorer," he said to himself.

Looking left and right, angling his head around from side to side, he was finally able to see the true panorama. It was clear he was at the summit of a large hill. The edges dropped away at a steady slope, brown dust ground kicking up little whirlwinds. The horizon stretched away in the distance to the right, with mountains hundreds of kilometres away from him. He could see in the middle distance herds of giant horned animals, their grey hides glinting in the sun. He stared at them as long as he could.

Those are bigger than elephants .
They look like dinosaurs.
Alien dinosaurs.

The horns were set on the tops of their heads and stretched along the ridge of their backs. His eyes could not take in any more detail, but Geoff was quite glad the herds were not near him. To the left of the gnarly red tree was an entire forest of red gnarly trees. Geoff could see over their tops so he was able to appreciate the size of this massive forest. Then slowly, Geoff looked down. He was only a step away from the ground, a brown dusty mud. Essentially, the portal was a perfect lookout point, although of course it could not face the other direction.

You could always find out if you went through.

He relaxed and put his hands on the portal's border. He expected it to act as a stable window but the bottom slipped away from him. He pulled back before he totally lost his balance and took a stepped away. The portal, pushed by the force exerted by Geoff's arms, widened in a matter of moments until it was twice as large, before slowing to a stop. Now it was wide enough to walk through. In fact, as far as Geoff could tell, the bottom lip of the portal ran through the floor of the school. He looked around the classroom fearfully, wondering if the building was about to collapse on him. Nothing happened. He looked back at the portal.

He texted Anne.

Come to my classroom after school.

He thought for a moment then texted her again.

Bring water and some snacks. We are going on a trip.

10
EXPLORATION

The two teachers were both behind the black curtain, staring out. The other sun was now in the sky although hidden from view, its rays causing the red tree to cast a shadow. The giant herd had become a dust cloud of movement. The occasional tail or head was visible but it was hard to distinguish the individual creatures. In their world, the sun was setting, the tower's long shadow cast over the classroom's side, darkening the already grime-obscured view.

"What are they?" said Anne.

"Big and fast and many. That's the bad. They are also far away, which is the good. Are you ready to step out?" Geoff had on his satchel and was making sure he had his packets of crisps and water inside. He listened for any sound from the rest of the school. Perhaps they had thought he had already gone home.

"Are you sure it's safe?"

"Not at all."

"Come on, man!"

"Hey, I don't know. I can breathe in there and my skin didn't melt in the what, two minutes I was exposed. But I don't know. Is there radiation? Earthquakes? How cold is it at night? Snakes?"

"Snakes?"

"There could be snakes."

"I don't like snakes."

"Me neither. Are you ready to step out?"

"Absolutely. Should we leave a note?"

"I think they'll work it out."

"They?"

"Whoever comes looking for us. This curtain is not exactly the most secure of holdings. Can we go now?"

"Sure." Anne took a deep breath. "Bye Earth." She took Geoff's hand. He looked down at it and then looked ahead.

They walked through the portal. And fell down a foot onto the ground. Geoff had forgotten to tell Anne about that first step, and she had pulled him down with her stumble. Anne looked at Geoff who shrugged his shoulders and took a deep lungful of air. Anne nodded and breathed in.

"Well, we're in it now," said Anne. She turned around and sat up to look at the portal. She tugged anxiously at Geoff's hand. He turned around to see what she was pointing at. The portal itself showed the black of the curtain. However it was what lay beyond the portal that made them gasp.

The land beyond the hill was a series of undulating plains. They could see far off into the distance due to the clear air. The purple sky was eerie but not unpleasant. There was not a cloud anywhere. The sun was huge and covered the sky with a red light. All along the plains they could see teeming wildlife. Herds of small and big animals, all of them utterly alien, challenged the eye and the mind with a plethora of colour and movement.

Something twinkling in the distance drew their eye. A superstructure -- a shiny building towered over the vista -- dominating it. Even at this distance of more than a hundred miles, Geoff could see this was much larger than any structure he had seen on Earth. The image was enough to make them stare in silence for what felt like forever.

Their reverie was broken by loud squawking. A flight of birds had taken up residence within the gnarly red tree. They now started with a cacophony of sound. As the teachers whirled around to face this surprise, one of the birds launched itself off the tree and at Anne. She screamed as its small crimson beak aimed straight for her face. The bird froze in mid-air, wings suddenly flapping no more. It fell to the ground, dead. As Anne looked where the bird had been a moment before, her eyes focused behind and on the tree. There stood Blue, smiling. He waved at them and ran along the tree branches before jumping off and rolling along the ground. He came to a stop at the feet of Geoff and did a perfect Finger Gun salute. Geoff responded in kind.

"Who showed him that?" laughed Anne.

"I think he saw me doing it. I sometimes greet my kids with it. Other times, I high five them. He did that to me as well."

The three of them turned together and looked at the vista. The black of the circular rift, edged by the blue shimmer, formed a half eclipse of the large red sun and the distant tower was framed by the surrounding landscape. It was a pleasing vista; Geoff felt no particular rush to return to his life. In fact, for the first time in a long time, he felt relaxed.

Would anyone know if I stayed here?

Who else is going to find out?

How big is this portal going to get?

Are you really going to just sit on your arse all day?

Geoff walked down the hill, the tower miles in front of him. As he got about thirty feet away from the rift, he knelt down in the ground. He picked up some of the dusty dirt and let it play out through his fingers. It looked like the ground back in his parents' garden. In fact, despite all the colours being different, the textures were practically identical for all the geographical terrain. The dead bird's feathers, the bark of the tree, the ground, even the brown grass, all had an unshakeable memory for Geoff, just as long as he closed his eyes as he touched them.

He turned round and looked up the steep incline at Anne and Blue. They were sat down surveying the scene. Anne was munching on a samgakgimbap, the seaweed wrap and glutinous rice a refreshing snack in the midday sun. As she ate, she pointed at everything that caught her eye and said its name slowly and repeatedly. Blue nodded happily and ate the dead bird, feathers and all.

I cannot believe she is still teaching.
No.
She is still attempting First Contact.

Anne pointed at the mountains. "Mountains. Mounnnnn- tins. Mounnnnn-tins." She looked expectantly at Blue. Blue nodded at her and swallowed the last of the bird. He licked his paws and pointed at the mountains. He opened his mouth, then after a moment closed it again. Anne sighed.

"That's okay, Blue," she said. "Take your time. There's no rush. I can wait."
Blue started drawing in the dust. Geoff came up the hill.

"Still not getting anywhere?" he asked Anne. She sighed and shrugged her shoulders.

"Sometimes, it takes time. I just can't get angry or impatient or emotionally invested."

"Sounds tough."

"Teaching isn't an easy gig. It doesn't start becoming easier just because it's in a different country."

"Or another planet."

"Right. I think he actually understands everything I am saying."

"Maybe he can't speak."

"That's what I thought at first, too. But he opens his mouth every so often, and then closes it again. I think he has the capacity for speech, but he's not confident."

"Maybe he's just mimicking your motion, the same way he mimicked my high fives."

"Maybe. Maybe, you're right." She conceded the point softly, looking away to Blue who was still drawing in the sand. She looked at what he was drawing.

"Maybe not." She stood up slowly and walked up behind Blue. Geoff came and joined her. The picture was a rough, if accurate drawing of the vista. Next to each recognizable part of the terrain Blue had written out its name. 'Mowtin' , 'Sun' , 'Ski'.

Anne knelt down and gently corrected the spelling errors. Blue watched her and nodded. She looked at him and pointed at the corrected words.

Blue sat down and rewrote the corrected words, carefully following the same strokes
that Anne used to make the characters. Then he wrote the next message

I can't speak. But I no English.

"You know English? You understand everything I say?" said Anne.
Blue smiled. Geoff pursed his lips.

"How long have you understood what we've said?" demanded Geoff.
Blue shrugged his shoulders and wrote in the dirt.

All the time.

"And you didn't tell us? What the hell, man?" said Geoff angrily. Blue looked scared and backed away. "No, don't you run away again!"

"Geoff!" Anne's shocked voice made Geoff turn on Anne.

"What?! He made us run around like idiots. Idiots! I changed my whole lesson plans just to communicate with him. And he understands everything. Everything!"

Sorry. The message was the result of a blur of motion. Blue looked up at Geoff, ears downcast.

"Oh he's sorry. He's sorry!" This was shouted out towards the tower, towards the sun and towards the portal. Geoff threw his hands up and kicked the ground angrily. He stormed off down the hill.

So much for being an astronaut.
More like a lab rat.

Anne watched him walk off and mutter to himself. She decided to let him blow off steam for a while. She turned back to Blue who was looking anxiously at Geoff.

"Why can't you speak?" asked Anne.
Blue pointed at the tower. Anne pursed her lips and narrowed her eyes toward the tower. Then he wrote:

You are not the first here.

The words in the dust raised the hackles on Anne's spine. She reached into her backpack reflexively.

"That tower is … bad?"

Blue nodded slowly, his solemn gaze never leaving Anne's.

Anne nodded at him. "Okay. Time to go home now." She shouted at Geoff who. behind the portal, gesticulated wildly. "Geoff! Let's get home! Now!"

Geoff turned around to respond to her shouting. Before he could say anything, Anne had started to run away from the portal down the other side of the hill. Blue jumped up and into the gnarly tree. There was a loud electrical sound and Blue fell out of the tree, motionless. Geoff ran halfway up the hill when he heard another electrical retort and Anne crying out in pain. He fell to the ground, still halfway up the hill. Out of the air, a black figure appeared landing on the ground and running away from Geoff. Geoff inched closer until he was just a few feet behind and under the portal. Another figure and another figure leapt out. They were all dressed in black with riot gear and strange rifles. They disappeared on the other side of the hill, then came back into view for a split second as they jumped back into the portal. Two of them were carrying the slumped form of Anne and one of them carried Blue.

Within a moment, Geoff was alone on an alien planet.

11
RELEASE

Geoff got up cautiously and stood against the side of the portal. He listened carefully. There was no sound at all. He looked sideways at the portal, only a sliver of Earth showed from his viewpoint. He was about to jump back into his classroom when a stick poked through from the other side.

Not a stick.
A gun.

Of course there was a sentry standing guard. There was a whole other planet waiting to invade. South Korea already had a pretty bad history with its neighbours attacking, invading and colonizing it over the last 1000 years. South Korea had the world's largest minefield as its wall against North Korea, a country more than half starved and run by an indolent spoiled child. Geoff could only guess what the reaction would be to an increasingly large opening in the middle of one of its largest cities to an entire alien planet. Geoff thought for a moment.

That portal does not just stop at the classroom.
Stop thinking in just two dimensions.

He crawled back down the hill, careful to make as little noise as possible. He was now behind the portal, so it was invisible to him.

But you know it's there.
It's behind you.
Oh no it isn't!

He then slid up under the portal. From this angle he could see the outline of the blue shimmer, a tiny elector snake in the middle of the air. He reached up and grabbed it. His fingers touched metal as the floor met the ceiling of the lower level. His fingertips slid on the metal, then his nails connected with a sill, a tiny shelf of energy that thrummed and vibrated through his knuckles.

As he pulled down the portal came with him. It widened in a circular fashion. There was a gasp and a shout, an American accent.

"Sir! The thing just got bigger!"

Americans.
That explains the guns.

Geoff pulled himself forward of the portal so he was on the entry side. As he looked at the bottom lip, it was now on the floor beneath the *hagwan*. Geoff rolled into it and fell heavily onto the floor five feet beneath.

"Thank you, low Korean ceilings," grunted Geoff. He got up and looked around. He was in the old dance studio. This had been a dance academy in more prosperous times. Now it was empty, cold and spooky.

This is the safest place I can think of right now.

He looked around and flinched each time he saw his shadowy reflection in the wall mirrors set all around the large room. The floor looked dusty but there were a number of footprints.

Not as abandoned as I thought.

Geoff inspected the whole floor, the darkness cut by the city lights. These windows had been cleaned from the outside and for the first time, Geoff was able to appreciate the view from his school tower.

Daegu is really very pretty in a Godzilla playing Dominoes kind of way.

Geoff slowly walked to the door to the stairwell and to the elevator. He looked up and down the stairwell. He decided he did not want to take the elevator and jogged down the stairs, his heart thumping wildly. As he got to the ground floor, he looked for flashing lights but did not see anything. He ducked behind a wall.

"Those guys did not come in a police car," he murmured. He flashed another look and saw two black vans parked about fifty metres up the road facing north. There did not appear to be any danger coming from the other side of the road so Geoff walked south, putting his hoodie up until he was around the corner of the road. He stopped, turned round and leaned against the wall, watching the building and the vans. He reached for his smartphone. He looked at his Contacts list. He had a total of two phone numbers: Mr. Kim and Anne.

See, this is why you should have more friends.

Mr. Kim was worse than useless. He simply was not an option. He rang Anne. It rang four times then was picked up.

"Hi Anne, are we still on for tonight?" he said in a bright cheery voice.

"No Anne-uh. Wrong Number."

Geoff clenched his jaw in suppressed anger.

They took his friends.
And put on a fake Korean accent!

Something snapped in his brain. All the pressure, all the stress, all the worry, all the mockery, it all suddenly combined and formed a stabbing white light in his mind. He walked towards the vans. He walked up to a corner of the street where people dropped off their trash. There were chairs, wardrobes and big white bags of garbage. There was also a baseball bat.

Liars.
Bullies.
Ruse.
Yes, that'll do nicely.

Geoff picked up the bat and walked up to the two vans. He rang Anne again. He heard a familiar ringtone from the front van. He walked past the front van, looking in the front cab and noting there was no one in the front seat. He looked at the black van, again seeing no one in the driver's seat. The phone was answered by the faux male Korean voice again.

"Wrong Number, ass-hole-uh." Click.

Liar.

Geoff swung the baseball bat and knocked off the wing mirror. The driver jumped out immediately. He was a white, pimply youth dressed in all black but still definitely army issue. Geoff barked out a laugh and the soldier stiffened.

He's just a baby.
And I'm the Most Dangerous Man In England.

"Hey man, what the hell's your problem?" said the soldier.

You.
Everything.
You.

Geoff swung the bat and hit the boy in the knee. Something satisfying popped and the young soldier went down screaming.

YES!

Geoff opened up the side van door. Two more young soldiers were playing on their phones and their weapons were not anywhere near close to hand. For a brief moment, Geoff saw Anne bound and gagged, lying on her side facing away from him. He hit one in the head and then the other. Both fell down, comatose. Geoff saw red. Bright, blotchy, veiny red. All the frustration of the night, of the time in Korea, of the years spent in England threatened to come out of him. He imagined chopping wood through a fine red mist and it felt so right. He tightened the grip on his bat as he stared down at the bodies. The ringing in his ears just would not stop.

A face appeared through the red, a powder blue of smiles and eyes, pushing away the rushing and the pain.

Stop.

Geoff gasped and the red mist fell away. Anne was still facing away from him, but he could hear her sobbing. He found himself numbly nodding as he threw the bat away. He climbed in the van and ungagged Anne.

"They got Blue," she said.

"Let's get you out of here. Don't look past me. Just look at my eyes," said Geoff, still breathing heavily. They got out of the van. Geoff carefully shut the door as Anne looked fixedly onto the ground. There was a thick dark pool collected around her sneakers.

"Where's Blue?" asked Geoff.

"I don't know. They pushed me out of there pretty quick. I think they were going to ask him some questions. Geoff?"

"Yeah?"

"They think his name is Geoff. They kept saying Geoff at him. I think they heard me talking to you and thought I was talking to him."

"So, they don't know who I am?"

You could just slip away.

The thought was a betrayal so hard Geoff had to shake himself.

"What do we do, Geoff? What do we do?"

Geoff looked at his short friend. "You need to disappear tonight. Grab your passport and get home."

"Like hell I will! Let's try another plan please." The little lady looked up at Geoff, chin jutted out defiantly. Geoff looked down at her and nodded.

"Right. Let's call running away Plan B then." They turned to the *hagwan* and walked in. They got into the elevator. Geoff pressed the top button.

"So, what's Plan A?" wondered Anne. The door opened. Waiting for them on the other side were ten soldiers all pointing their guns at the two teachers. One of them had a walkie-talkie to his mouth and had just finished a conversation.

"My name is Geoff. I am who you are looking for. I just attacked your men outside. Tell your boss I am ready to fully co-operate."

Any way you want it.
I should have just slipped away.
Who told me to stop?

12
INTELLIGENCE

Major Jarrod Clegg rubbed his temples, and resisted the temptation to stab himself in the eyes with his own thumbs." It had been going so well," he thought to himself ruefully.

Everything about Clegg was stiff but perfectly coiffed like a high street mannequin. From the choice of wire frame glasses to his careful side parting, Major Clegg had always tried to be a bit of a clothes horse, although he would of course strenuously deny such an accusation. When he was a fresh cadet, he would, and frequently did look like a scared schoolboy. Now in his early fifties, his eyelids drooped a little but otherwise he maintained his stiff demeanour from all those years ago.

Having worked the system well, Clegg had been fast tracked up the promotions ladder until he found himself with the plum job working in the JSA. Working the Border of North Korea was, in the Major's opinion, the most patriotic thing any American could do. Protecting your people from the Northern menace came naturally to the Major and he had worked the border for the past decade. Other men might have wondered if the military bigwigs had forgotten about him but Major Clegg was sure they had recognised his talents. Then one night, he had been summoned to a meeting in Seoul. He arrived and was ushered into an empty warehouse. There, he had found his orders in a 'For Your Eyes

71

Only" package.

He was shown power signatures escalating in Daegu. He was told there was an unknown quantity to these power signatures and that he was to be sent along with a small team to investigate. Although no one mentioned it to him at all, he was quite sure they were talking about North Korean nuclear weapons. He drove down that night and set up base at a nearby warehouse. His orders had made it clear he was not to go through official channels and to stay off military frequencies. Clegg agreed; there were Northern spies everywhere even, sadly, in the army.

Within a day he had worked out the insurgent was a deep sleeper named Kim who ran an English Academy as a front. The power signature was located in the classroom run by the foreign teacher. Clegg was not sure if the British man was also a spy or simply ignorant of the danger he was in. He was well aware how stupid most hippy teachers were. The TEFL teachers were an embarrassment to the Western Hemisphere whose very existence threatened to undermine the resolve of his glorious troops. However, the Englishman constantly met with an American who could have been his handler. That made the British man a CIA stoolie and Clegg was damned if that agency would get there before him.

Major Clegg sped up his operation accordingly. When they burst through the doors of the *hagwan*, they found Mr. Kim snoring like a pig. Throwing him to the ground, his handpicked commandos, his most loyal troops, tied the school director up and ran on to the final room. Major Clegg strolled in behind his men, smiling at a plan well-executed. As he walked into the foreign teacher's room, he saw the subtle subterfuge. The spies had thought to create a false wall, a fake partition but Kim was wise to their ruse.

He could hear their conversation.

"Geoff! Time to leave! Now!"

They were planning to escape the country. Kim was not going to let that happen. He ripped away their intricate curtain to reveal the truth.

He stared.

The foreigners had invented a portal to North Korea. The pollution must be worse than presupposed. The sky was purple for heaven's sakes! Regardless, his way lay clear. Capture the spies and secure the breach. North Korea could not enter the South through his watch, that was for damn sure.

"Arrest them both!" the command was sharp and the response sharper. Within seconds his men had disappeared unwaveringly into the energy source and then came back with the American woman and the British man. The British man had suffered terribly through continued exposure to the nuclear device. As he gazed upon his shrunken, blue form, Major Kim took a step back. He did not want that to happen to his elegant features.

"This is the Englishman?" asked the Major. One of his men looked at him with poorly hidden dismay.

"Uh, no sir, that's an animal. Possibly an alien. From the alien planet sir."

"Alien planet?"

"Yes sir, that over there appears to be an alien planet."

"I see. And what's your name soldier?"

"Jennings, sir, Private First Class." The Major gave him a patented, withering look. The Private had the gall to remain unmoved by this eyeball. Clegg was quite sure Jennings was going to be patrolling the Yukon by the end of the month. He inspected the portal view again.

"Soldier, do you mean to tell me this is an alien planet?" He gestured to the panorama.

"Yes, sir. And that is an alien life form."

"Aliens aren't blue, boy! They're grey!"

"Avatar was blue."

73

"Avatar was a goddamn movie!"

"Sir, yessir!" The CIA handler was staring at the exchange open-mouthed. She looked awfully young to be a spy. Major Kim decided she would need to be deported.

"Send her to the warehouse, we'll let Langley know we have one of theirs and let them deal with her. This guy, this 'alien', is staying with me to answer some questions."

The young woman spoke. "You're in charge here?"

"You're damn right, Missy."

"Wow. How did that happen?" The Major noted how Jennings smiled at that. The Yukon was becoming ever more present in this young man's future. Clegg sent her off and planned his interrogation.

Thirty minutes later, Major Clegg cursed the development. It had all seemed to be going so well. The alleged alien was bred and moved to a secure location. The CIA operative was at his base of operations. Now this woman had reappeared with her British man, and they were both claiming to be teachers. The man was clearly in Special Ops. How else could he have beaten his men, who he had been personally assured were the best Camp Walker had offered? Major Clegg looked at his soldiers. They had been beaten badly, and by all accounts, by just this one teacher. He gave them his worst scowl of disapproval and returned to his paperwork and let them stand there uncomfortably. He held a piece of paper in his delicate hands. How could he have slipped through his tight security ring not once but twice?

The 'teachers' also claimed the portal was to a different world. Kim could feel the eye roll from Jenkins, even though the young soldier was behind him. He deigned to not respond to the eyeroll of insubordination. They also claimed the blue creature was an alien. Major Kim took another look at the ugly thing, currently in a box crate in the adjacent classroom. It looked like, in the Major's considered opinion, someone had spray-painted a koala and put it on a fitness regime. The Major was not impressed.

He ordered all three arrested, including the Korean director. None of them offered any kind of objection, although the Korean had pissed himself and wailed like a goddamn baby. Clegg knew better than to fall for that. The North Koreans were the elite at subterfuge. He would not have been surprised if the urine had turned out to be a goddamn WMD.

They had been sent to the warehouse and now he was stuck with his slightly bruised and battered troops. He decided a little paperwork might be in order. Firstly, he checked their military record. He was not pleased with their results. Apart from Jennings, who was clearly a rabble rouser, and Levinson, who was a Jew, none of them had any battle experience. In fact, twelve of the sixteen had enlisted only six months previously. He sent a message through to his mysterious chain of command. They had still not deigned to tell him exactly who they were. He mentioned detaining the operatives but decided to leave out the problematic portal. He decided he would investigate it first so he would actually have something to report. Writing down the words 'mysterious portal of unknown origin' did not seem like a good idea.

"Men," he said, "Men, let's go talk to these people." He noticed those bruised privates seemed particularly eager to have a conversation.

13
SHELVED

Geoff woke up in blinding pain. He struggled against his bonds and opened his eyes. He felt something tear on his face and realised it was his skin. The soldiers had not liked being made a fool of and once he had been dumped in the warehouse, Geoff had been worked over pretty well.

It's almost like the people who were hitting you had been attacked by you on a previous occasion.
Shut up.

Now he was alone in a room, tied to a chair and a light shining above him. Blood caked one side of his face and he could feel the beginnings of a black eye. No one had asked him a question.

No one cares.
You do it to yourself, you do.

As he stared blearily around his confines, a door opened behind him.

"What the hell is this? Who told you to do this to him? He's a goddamn teacher!"

"Get off my ass, Jennings. Major said he was a spy. Figured we would find out what he knew."

"Who told you to do that? Untie him."

"You're not my boss."

"Untie him *now*." Geoff felt someone behind him and his bonds loosen. He got up and gingerly rubbed his eye and chin. He looked at the two soldiers. One of them came towards him.

"I'm sorry about this, sir, he's a punk kid, I would take him out back and teach him a lesson, but I'm worried he would fail that lesson as well."

Geoff tried to smile through cracked lips. "I expect he will learn the error of his ways."

That's right, act like you've been here before.
Try not to shit yourself.
"Where are my friends?"

"The Korean and the American lady are in the next room. We have a few questions for you."

"The Korean? Mr. Kim? He doesn't know anything."

Neither do you.
But this guy doesn't know that.

"Where is Blue?"

"The alien? He is secure."

What the hell does THAT mean?

"Can I see them please?"

"I want to ask a few questions first."

"Individually, then as a group."

77

Teacher humor.
Your friend is not the only one failing lessons.
Damn, this is starting to be fun.
What is wrong *with me?*

"Sorry, sir?" the soldier had maintained a level of polite rebuttal throughout the conversation. Geoff had done a biology experiment when he was younger, cutting up a rat and looking at each element of its dietary tract. Geoff was starting to feel like that rat.

"We do the opposite with our classes. First as a group, then as individuals."

"How long you been a teacher?"

"Three months."

"That's a small amount of time. What did you do before?"

"Temp work, sewage response, office work. Nothing really."

I was The Most Dangerous Man In England, no big deal.

"And how do you know Miss Henson?"

"Who?"

"Your 'friend'."

"Anne? We met in the bar here."

And I don't know her.
She's my closest friend and I don't know her.

"And Mr. Kim?"

"He's my boss."

"And….." Jennnings paused expectantly at Geoff. Geoff sighed.

"Blue. His name is Blue. He's from the other planet and he is a good guy."

"Blue?"

"Anne named him when we thought…"

"…Yes?"

When we realized he was a smarter guy than all you lot put together.

"Nothing."

"You named him when you thought he was…." The question hung in the air for a while, then the soldier smiled at Geoff with kind eyes and nodded. Then he got up. "I understand. You want to protect your people."

"Who are you? You know my name and Anne's name and Mr. Kim. I don't know who you are."

"Private First Class Jennings. Andrew Jennings."

"And you're working for the Major?"

"That is the notion." Jennings smiled. "I apologise for what happened to you and your friends. I hope it doesn't happen again."

With that Jennings got up and left Geoff alone in his room.

Alone at last.
Did he even lock the door?
I suppose I am meant to assume I am being watched.
That there is a guard right outside my room.
I suppose I am meant to feel scared.
Bugger that.

Geoff walked to his door and turned the handle. He opened the door slowly and looked outside. There was no one there.

Perhaps they don't rate you a threat.
Give me a baseball bat.

He walked out of the large room into a much bigger warehouse. Giant shelves rising high to the distant ceiling formed long corridors. When Geoff came to an intersection he looked down one way and saw double doors. He walked towards them, but before he could get any closer, he heard voices ahead. He ducked into a side corridor and walked slowly towards the sound. Looking though the metal shelf, which held some sort of farming equipment, Geoff could go without being seen.

I am ninja.

Anne was sat down on a chair, and was being questioned by a man in uniform. It was the man who had seemed in charge of the soldiers at the *hagwan.*The man looked older and more senior than Jennings, and he seemed quite agitated.

"So you're telling me, Miss Henson," the man drawled languorously in some sort of Southern American accent, "you have managed to discover a whole planet by accident? And that you chose to do this on foreign territory?"

This guy has watched too many police dramas.

"I don't know if you can choose an accident," began Anne but the man cut her off.

"Well, that's just not patriotic, Miss Henson. How long have you hated your country?"

"I don't hate my country."

"You haven't lived there for seven years, and you just renewed your visa. You're staying here for another year. Seems to me, maybe you could have discovered this place just to not go back to America. Seems to me, you're being ridiculous."

Ridiculous, says the jumped up peacock.

80

He's verbally attacking a handcuffed teacher, and he looks half terrified at the prospect.
I don't think he knows the meaning of the word.

Anne sighed and jutted out her chin as she responded. "I love my country but there are no jobs. I didn't plan on discovering anything. My friend said there was a creature in his classroom and I went to help him find it. I have to get to work in the next twenty minutes and if you don't let me get to it, I'm going to be late. Please, I'm an American citizen. You have no legal recourse to hold me like this. Let me go."

"This creature, this is the tame creature, the one you call Blue? Tell me more about him."

"Where is he?"

"Somewhere safe."

"Safe for who, Major? Are you going to say America? I bet you're going to say America."

Damn girl.
You are stone cold.
Here you are, handcuffed, in trouble with the US Army.
But you seem just fine.
Where the hell you been?

"Good afternoon, Miss Henson." The man got up.

"So can I go to work?" The Major walked to the door. "I am going to take that silence as a yes. Walk through that door if you mean yes." The door clicked closed. Geoff was about to get up and help Anne when she changed her demeanor. She went from relaxed to alert, from docile to looking around the room in a covert manner. She then jerked her head round until she was looking directly at Geoff. She smiled broadly, easily but Geoff felt she was hiding something.

"Oh, hi there, Geoff. Are you just going to hide in the shadows or help out a lady in distress?" Geoff got up and walked out of his hiding place.

So much for being ninja.

She smiled at him as he came out of the shadows. "Glad to see you, man." Her smile faltered as she saw his face. "I see they worked you over pretty good."

"I was worried they were going to do the same to you," said Geoff gruffly.

"You're very sweet. We need to hurry. The Major has Blue somewhere and we need to retrieve him as soon as possible." Geoff came to Anne's knots. As he touched them, they seemed to just fall away and Anne stood up.

"Well done," said Anne. Geoff stared at the small coil of rope. They had been practically hanging off Anne's wrists. He looked at her confusedly. Anne had the decency to look embarrassed.

"Would you believe large wrists, small hands?"

"Not really, no."

"Well, we don't really have time for this. We have to follow the Major." Anne walked to the door and Geoff followed after her, thoughts whirling through his head.

Where is Blue?
How much trouble am I in?
Anne knows way more than she is letting on.
Don't trust her.

14
RETURN

The door led to another doorway and that led to the outside. Somehow it was still dark. Traffic was nonexistent on the suburban road. All the businesses in the area were closed, either for the day or forever. Either way, the road was a wall of corrugated iron shutters.

Geoff looked for his phone but it had been taken by the soldiers.

"I don't suppose you still have your phone on you, do you?" he asked.

"Uh, yeah," muttered Anne and she pulled it out. She looked at it for a moment then looked down one direction of the road.

"That way," and set off. She had chosen the way that was slightly more downhill. In Daegu's constantly undulating terrain, that probably would not last long but Geoff was tired and thankful.

Remember, don't trust her.

"What's the time?" he asked her back.

"Six thirty in the morning. Amazingly, we could find Blue, escape from the soldiers and still have you be on time for your classes."

Geoff smiled to himself. "I don't think they are going to let me back in that classroom. I don't think they're going to let anyone in that *hagwan*."

"You're right." Anne stopped and sighed. She turned around to Geoff. He could see tired regret in her eyes. "Look, you should probably think about going back to England. If those guys find you again, there's no telling what they may do to you. Do you have enough money saved up?"

Geoff recoiled at her words, the same words he had said to her only a few hours before. The very idea of leaving her alone now seemed so cowardly, so dishonourable.

So easy to slip away.
Blue!
Coward.

The insidious thought was hammered away by his rage. His friend needed him. His friends needed him. He walked past her and turned around, talking to her as he walked backwards.

"I'm not going anywhere. I have enough money to survive until I find another job." He smiled at a thought. "I don't see Mr. Kim giving me a bad reference. Teachers are always getting told to bring realia into the classroom, right. Well I brought a whole planet. Jobs will flood in. Let's go find Blue together."

Anne smiled wryly back at him, then looked at her phone again. "This way," and walked up an intersection. Geoff slowed and followed her. His eyes narrowed.

"How do you know where the Major went?" asked Geoff.

"I put a tracker on your phone, and the Major has that right now." Anne had now walked on beyond Geoff, who once more came to a stop.

"Okay. Obviously my next question has to be 'when did you put a tracker on my phone?'" Anne did not respond. Geoff shook his head and ran to keep up with her. Once he was level with her, he glared at her for a while but they kept walking on in silence. Then, she smiled and stopped.

"I cannot believe this guy," she said and pointed. Geoff looked. They had somehow, through all the little alleyways and byways, ended up right back at the *hagwan*.

"It's like it's the nexus of all journeys. All roads lead to my *hagwan*," said Geoff sarcastically.

"Maybe," murmured Anne. She turned and looked at Geoff, a calculating glint in her eye. "How did you get back from the planet anyway? They placed a guard over the portal." Geoff looked pointedly at her.

Don't trust her.
Don't trust her.
Blue.

Geoff explained how the bottom lip of the portal hung down below the floor of the *hagwan* and below the ceiling of the dance academy beneath. Anne smiled.

"So we can still go into the portal? Let's go get some coffee from the shop. Then maybe you can take me dancing, if you know what I'm saying." She waggled her eyebrows.

Girls don't use that expression right.
Or, maybe they do and we are doing it horribly wrong.
That makes a lot more sense.

She then looked both ways and crossed the street to the tower. Geoff was only a half step behind her. When they got to the front entrance, Geoff noted the black vans parked outside and tugged his hoodie closely over his head.

The two teachers went up the stairs to the ninth floor, where the cafe was still open, and the two baristas were now asleep with their heads on the counter. The portal glimmered, a small shimmering sliver about a foot-high running along the border of the cafe's ceiling. The schoolgirl was nowhere to be seen although her books were still strewn all over the table. Anne looked at the books then looked around.

"Must be in the bathroom. If we're going to go, we should go now." The portal shimmered slightly but was no brighter than the flickering neon lights. If no one looked directly at it, or looked for it, it would be a part of the background of shiny glittering images that made up the coffee shop wall. Geoff boosted Anne up and into the portal space. She turned around and held out her hand. Geoff took it and lifted himself into the other planet. He turned around and pulled himself up using the girders within the building.

Look at me, climbing inside a building to another planet, avoiding the army of another country.
No big deal.

As he lifted himself he felt himself touching the rift with his back. It stretched and rolled away from him easily a couple of inches in all directions.

Don't want to be touching that too much.

He pulled himself through and laid down next to Anne, in the sunset shadow of the tall hill. They looked at each other and smiled, breathing in the arid air.

"Good to be back," said Geoff. Anne put a finger to her lips and pointed upwards. Geoff looked up and into the portal. He could see the ceiling of his classroom in the distance, and the edge of a rifle poking through. Geoff looked at the rift itself. It was even bigger. Now the sides had widened but the length had stayed the same, turning the circle into an oblong. Geoff could see the electrical wires and piping that was in the building, along with thick metal girders. Furthermore, he could see right along the edge of his classroom. When the portal continued growing, Miss Huang's classroom would also be accessible.

Anne nudged Geoff and pointed under the portal. Geoff nodded and they slowly and quietly shuffled down. When they were clear from view, they stood up. Anne stood on tiptoe to whisper in Geoff's ear. "My stuff is still up there, I bet. Yours too. Let's go get it and make a plan."

They headed around the hill, until their ascent would not be spotted by the portal's sentries. They scrambled up the dusty incline in silence, and Geoff was thankful his smoking days were behind him. Calling this a hill was fair, since it was only about four hundred feet high. Still, the going was tough and Geoff was thankful when they made the summit. Anne looked around worriedly.

"Where's our stuff?" Geoff looked around as well. Everything, from Geoff's backpack to Anne's picnic blanket had gone. Geoff looked around the vista, hands on his hips, as if by staring he could magic their belongings back into existence. Anne nudged him.

"Do you hear that? The birds have gone quiet."

When he listened for the birds' inane chatter, he realized she was right. Then he heard two very different sounds, each setting his teeth on edge and his skin on fire.

The roar of an enraged animal and the scream of a teenage girl.

Geoff and Anne both started instinctively running towards the sounds, coming from over the lip of the summit.

This cannot be a good idea.
Who runs to a scream and a roar?

Looking down, they saw a dreadful sight. A small Korean girl, still wearing her school uniform was crumpled on the floor, holding a bleeding leg. Geoff recognised her.

From the dance room. She's the one in the poster.

About thirty paces away and slowly moving from side to side was a terrifying apparition of a creature. It resembled a giant cat in its movements, but its mane was a dusky red. The rest of its body was a bony white hide. It roared at the girl again, thrusting its giant head towards her, its yellow eyes glowing, its immense curved teeth forming a giant steel trap. The creature was about the size of a school bus.

There's no way we can stop that thing.

That girl is dead.
We should probably get out of here.
She might slow it down.

"She has our stuff!" said Anne indignantly, and strode down the hill towards the creature.

Or we can do that.

Anne shouted at the monstrous being. "You want some of this, buddy?"

The shouting drew the creature's attention and it swung its head round to face this new challenge. Geoff remained frozen to the spot as he watched his friend walk into certain death.

15
GUN

Geoff watched on as Anne started shouting at the girl in fluent, furious, Korean. Geoff had no idea what was being said but by judging Anne's incredulous face and wagging finger, the Korean girl was taking an immense ticking off. The monster growled menacingly at Anne and she immediately shouted back, raising her arms and trying to be big. The monster skipped back a few steps and roared again. By the time this had happened, Anne's purposeful step had allowed to reach the prostrate teen. Anne slapped her hard across the face and grabbed her bag from the girl's shoulders. Geoff watched everything from his frozen position on the hill.

Well, at least I am safe here.

Anne pointed at Geoff and shouted at the girl. The girl struggled to her feet.

Oh no.

Anne reached into her bag, checking the items inside, then grabbed Geoff's satchel and pushed the girl towards the Englishman. The girl broke into a shambling gait, her injured leg obviously hampering her progress.

No.

The monster roared and charged at the girl.

NONONONONONO!

"Move!" he shouted. The girl redoubled her efforts. The monster slewed between Anne and the schoolgirl, its back legs scrabbling to find purchase. It churned the ground under it before powering forward. For a moment, it looked like the monster would trip up but its heavy, clawed feet dug in and its leg muscles coiled, ready for the final pouncing move. Geoff could see every fine detail on the girl's face, from the flecks of sweat, to the acne-riddled reddened cheeks, to the eyes wide with terror. Time slowed as he saw the animal rise up behind her, its two front legs raised out in a gruesome crucifix of predation.

A shot rang out and the animal's trajectory altered every so slightly. Now it spun in the air, torpedoing toward the girl. As it fell, another shot rang out. The monster's arms windmilled crazily before landing, crashing into the incline and rolling over itself. Behind it, Geoff saw Anne still holding the weapon in her hand.

That is the biggest pistol I have ever seen in my whole life.

She trembled slightly as she remained in her fixed position.

The animal crashed into the girl. She screamed as she disappeared under the pile of moving flesh and hide. Anne put the outsized weapon back into her backpack and swung that onto her shoulder. She ran to the dead monster and started lifting up one arm at a time.

"Help me!" She shouted at Geoff.

"You shot it!"

"Help me!" She was becoming frantic in her effort.

"You have a gun! What the hell, Anne?" Geoff was shouting back now. Anne stopped wrestling with the dead legs and started towards Geoff, her face a mask of rage. Geoff took a step back involuntarily. Anne stopped and with a clear conscious attempt at control, took a deep breath.

"We can talk about this after. Right now there is a little girl dying under there. She's dying, Geoff! Please, for the love of Christ, help me."

They stood still for a moment looking at each other. Geoff walked down past Anne, his shoulder pushing her out of the way.

Love of Christ.
Well, I'm Jewish.
Forgive me.
That's what I should have said.

He bent down to the carcass and lifted with his knees. Anne pushed with him, then ducked down and grabbed the unconscious girl's hand. She yanked at it and the torso slid out. Another yank and the girl suddenly came free and Anne collapsed down next to her. Geoff dropped the carcass down and felt for the girl's pulse.

"Alive," he said, wheezing and falling down away from the two women. Anne leaned over the girl's body.

"She's breathing." The American said. Geoff looked up. The sun threw out flares across the sky. For the first time, Geoff saw a wisp of a cloud. He pointed at it.

"Looks like rain," and smiled. Anne giggled.

"A deluge, most likely," she replied and they both laughed. Geoff leaned over to Anne.

"You're not just here to teach, are you?" He said. It was not a question. Anne stared at the sky.

"I really am a great teacher. I work very hard at my job. I'm probably one of the best in this city. Seoul might have better but, honestly, fuck Seoul."

91

"Anne-"

"Geoff, can I just say you are a most remarkable man. Here you are, on an alien planet you discovered, having made first contact, the first contact ever of a sentient being. You have survived an alien atmosphere, an alien gravity, hell, alien irradiation from an alien sun..." Anne faltered. She was still staring at the sky.

Geoff waited for a moment. "What's your point?"

"A girl can do more than one thing, okay?"

Geoff shook his head. They both sat there in silence for a while, the Korean girl lying between them, the dead body of a monster meters away, the red sun shining down on them.

Work starts in three hours .
There's a teenager missing from her home.
A Major has kidnapped my alien friend.
The only friend who can help me is a liar with a gun.
Man, I hope I get fired.

16
COFFEE

Kim Ga Bin woke up and felt aches throughout her body. She groaned to herself. She had fallen asleep in the studio again. The girl closed her eyes and a flash of the nightmare she'd been having sent a jerk through her whole wrecked body. She blinked and a red crested roar echoed through her mind. She stood up suddenly and grabbed her books and papers off the floor. She thrust them haphazardly into her backpack.

Ga Bin would have to hurry if she was going to get to school on time. She had told her father she had a study group at her friend's house. He had believed her. Rather, her father never enquired deeply into his daughter's life. Most nights, she was in here, studying, or more likely, filming another YouTube video. She liked performing her own choreography. She hoped one of these videos would be noticed by a dance school and she could get a scholarship.

Her Kakao beeped at her. The messaging app was the only way she and her school friends communicated. They knew their parents would never look through their phone, so the planning of any illicit movement, such as Ga Bin's frequent sojourns occurred through the app. She was gone through the door and texting her friends furiously. Kakao dragged all thoughts of foreigners from her mind. Not looking where she was going, Ga Bin walked into a bannister and felt her leg bruise up quickly. She looked down and saw it already had drawn blood. She stared at the sight, trying to remember if any of her dance maneuvers had gone wrong the previous night. She couldn't recall doing any dancing last night. She bit her lip and resolved to up the dosage for her Ritalin. She sighed. It was not the first time she had not been able to recall portions of her life.

As she got to the ground floor, she realized she also had a pain on her ribs. She wondered at that. She slowed down at the tower entrance. She looked up uncertainly at the stairwell, and at the studio many flights above. She took a half step back toward the stairwell, but then her phone beeped again. She winced and answered it, walking out into the street.

Anne watched the bruised Korean girl limp away and turned to look back at Geoff. She blew her coffee and looked at her phone. The two teachers were sat down on the other side of the street, drinking steaming mugs of coffee on the balcony of the café.

"Okay, I think we get about thirty minutes before you got class. I would go to your *hagwan* and see if anyone is there. I have a feeling you won't be able to go in. Smile, nod, and ask for your pay check. They'll pay you and you can leave. We can always get in through there." She pointed up at the dance studio. She and Geoff had pulled a black curtain across the mirrored wall of the dance studio. As long as no one wanted to use that mirrored wall everything would be fine. He looked at Anne blowing on her coffee.

Now.
Ask her now before she's not your friend.

"I'm going to assume you're not FBI or a presidential secret service. I got you down to NSA or CIA but I'm not sure which. I'm leaning toward CIA but that's because I really like spy novels." He said all this calmly, even as his heart was pounding.

"Jack Ryan was NSA," said Anne, holding her cup with two hands, sipping, looking every inch a younger sister being told off by her older brother. Geoff did not buy her pose at all. The pounding had reached his ears.

Woman.

94

Ruse.
Fool.
Fool.

"Jack Ryan was not a spy, he was an analyst. If you're analyzing, please tell me what you're analyzing. What or who or why. I'll take any of those as answers. I'd also like to know how long you were going to keep pretending to be my friend. I'd also like to know if you were going to free yourself from that van. I'd also like to know-"

"If I was pretending to be your friend, I would have stopped that pretense now. I have inspected the asset and know the access points."

"The asset? You mean the portal?"

"Yes."

"The portal is the access point."

"Quite. When those guys tied me up, I was probably going to get beaten up before I would have got free. When you showed up and rescued me, I was thankful and relieved. I'm sorry it meant you got beaten up instead of me, and again I am thankful you took that for me. " For the first time a while, Anne looked directly into Geoff's eyes. In fact, Anne's eyes were the only part of her face he could see over her steaming mug. "This planet is a very big deal, you know that. You're not stupid. When England took control of the New World, it was a continent of untold riches, resources the Crown could not possibly have imagined. If America had not won its independence quickly and decisively, if France had not left the new country alone, if Spain had not focused its energy further south, America could have been, *should* have been a site of conflict for decades. Wars would have followed wars, hundreds of thousands of dead men. And that was just a continent! Now, we're talking about a planet. A freaking planet, man. At a time of overpollution, overpopulation, over extension of every form of resource, here is a planet that has the potential to fix all those problems to the lucky country that controls it. And you found it in Korea. A country that has North Korea and China looking in. One country led by a power-hungry dictator, another that has terrible over population, terrible human rights violations as its standard and terrible pollution."

95

"Don't forget America," Geoff replied, putting his cup down. "You have interests here. And it would not be the first time the U.S. has swooped in to grab what resources it can. You guys are the worst of the bunch!"

"Ask yourself, which of those four countries would you rather have keeping this situation stable? America is the only super power left. I know it's cool and easy to say we are the bad guys, the Roman Empire of our times, the bullies, whatever, but seriously. Seriously. You are faced with a choice of either South Korea, North Korea, China, or America. Who do you want in charge? No, Geoff, we may be fallible but we are nowhere near the worst." Anne got up and headed to the door. "And you know I'm right." She went downstairs. Geoff stayed sat down staring at his cup, mulling her words. Anne certainly seemed to have a handle on things. He was quite happy to leave her and the Major to it. There was only one problem that she seemed to have forgotten about.

Blue.
I'm coming to get you.

17
CLOSURE

Geoff waited a minute after Anne left. Then, he went up the stairs but stopped in the middle of the stairwell. Above him, he could hear a large argument breaking out. The vast majority of the shouting was in Korean, with a bit of English sprinkled in.

"Let us in," the voice of Miss Huang floated down to Geoff, quavering quite bravely above the hubbub. "I have to prepare classes today. My children arrive in fifty minutes."

"This academy is closed down by order of the government."

Which government?
Because you sure don't sound Korean.

An American voice, it sounded young and flint hard. Geoff could imagine the gun attached to that voice.

"You're not Korean. This is Korea!" An angry male voice, so Geoff knew it was not one of the teachers. He knew Mr. Kim's voice and this was not it. Geoff risked a peek through the stairwell. He could see a large group of angry Koreans. Just beyond the seething mass of humanity Geoff could see a line of soldiers fully decked out, right down to the cookie cutter camouflage uniform and large gleaming guns. Their leader held up his hand. He had severe bruising on his face.

Ah, I recognise you.
I think I recognise most of your friends as well.

The wall of soldiers had more than a smattering of black eyes and puffed up lips.

I should feel bad.
But I don't.

"I understand you are upset but you shouting will not change this situation. Until otherwise notified, this academy is shut down. You will receive your payments to this academy as parents, and you teachers will get your last month's wages sent to you. Now, I must ask you to leave the area. Please, for your own safety, leave this area."

"I'm calling the police," the Korean man snarled at the soldier, then pulled out his smartphone. "I'm calling the news. I'm calling everyone."

"Sir," sighed the soldier, "I cannot begin to tell you what a bad idea that would be. Listen, this is a matter of National Security. Let's just say it involves the North."
The crowd fell silent at this news. Geoff shook his head.

Oh no he didn't just use the N word!
Well, the other N word.

"Excuse me, sir, did I just hear you say there is a problem with North Korea? Is that why you and your men took me captive last night? Is that why you beat me up?" Geoff didn't even realize he had come up the stairs. As he walked to the crowd, the soldiers' familiar faces showed that, they too, remembered him very well. Geoff's pace slowed. Then he stopped, mid stride. The crowd ceased their susurration, their mob movement. The soldier stopped, his mouth half-formed into a response. The room darkened and Geoff could not see anything. Then, an image covered his expanse. It was Blue, his ears popped high, his eyes spinning like black whirlpools.

98

Blue!
I see you, man.
You're in a cage.
I am coming for you, Blue!

The poor guy was trapped in a plastic cage. He looked sad. In fact, Geoff was sure Blue was looking at him sadly. Geoff found himself getting lost in the detail of Blue's eyes. The image popped out as a gun barrel end entered and then dominated his eyesight. The crowd returned to its organic rhythm. The soldier's face completed its grotesque movement.

"You were told not to come back here," snarled the soldier.

Blue is in here.

"You need to leave," said the soldier. He had stepped right into Geoff's space. Spittle landed on the teacher's face. Geoff looked at him, tilting his head.

"Blue is in here," he said softly to the soldier.

"Who the hell is Blue?"

"Oh, you know. You know! Blue is in here and you have him in a cage." The soldier's eyes widened and then narrowed in anger.

"You need to leave now!"

Geoff felt an explosion go off in his stomach. He looked down as he fell and saw the rifle butt return to its position. As Geoff fell, groaning, there was a moment of silence. The soldiers looked at the thin crowd of parents and teachers. Then they stepped over Geoff and attacked the Koreans. From Geoff's angle, it looked like the soldiers would just move right through the crowd. Geoff saw Miss Huang get hit in the face and a spray of blood burst from her nose. She fell screaming and looked along the floor at Geoff. Geoff could only stare back numbly.

Sorry for using you.

Then the Korean men started hitting back. The soldiers were young and battle-trained. However, half of them had been assaulted with a baseball bat very recently. The Korean men were fit and had learned a range of close quarter martial arts. Their muscle memory in Tae Kwon Do, Hapkido and JiuJitsu found themselves responding. Their genetic memory saw an enemy in army uniform attacking their women and they responded. In the close confines and with orders to not even load their weapons, the soldiers suddenly found themselves in the battle of their lives. Knives and guns of young and dumb were dispatched by older, more trained, more capable hands.

Time to go.

Geoff crawled away from the fight.

No one ever notices.

He found himself in the foyer and he got up and stumbled down the corridor. His heart hammered in his chest and his breath was ragged. He moved with purpose to his classroom. He opened up the door and found the portal wide across the back wall. The alien rift lit up the room brightly. In the room itself, was an army phone system, a large backpack with an antenna attached. It looked lke something out of a Vietnam war movie and felt incongruous in its setting of children's pictures.

Geoff did not care about that. There was no sign of Blue. He exited and walked into Miss Huang's class. The portal continued on this side, stretching right across the wall. The electric blue shimmer was now a broad blue snake running down the middle of the room.

No one's hiding this anymore.
Good.

In the corner was a plastic cage, exactly how Geoff had seen it only a few moments before, right down to the black hinges. Blue was holding onto the front bars and smiling.

"It's like he absolutely knew I was coming for him right now," reflected Geoff. He thought on that as he looked for a way to open the cage. There had been no doubt in Geoff's mind that Blue was in the academy, no doubt that he was in the cage.

That's two times he's been in my head.
Maybe more.

Geoff stopped and grinned at Blue. "Been thinking about you Blue," he said to the creature who smiled back. "In fact, I've been wondering if all the thinking was my own." Blue's eyes whirled a dance of colours for a second, then he smiled back. Blue looked at the door in a concerned way. Geoff listened for a second. The fighting noises had dissipated. Geoff got up and risked a look around the doorway.

The soldiers had pushed the parents and teachers down the stairwell and had now locked the academy doors. With the soldiers on the inside, the angry Koreans were now pushing on the doors. This kept the attention of most of the soldiers but there was one who sitting against the wall, nursing a bloody face. As Geoff looked down the corridor, there was an awful moment where their eyes met. As the soldier started to react, Geoff ducked back into the room and grabbed the whole cage. He ran out, awkwardly hoisting the cage, and went into his classroom. The soldier had shouted an alarm but due to his bloody nose and the general mayhem no one had reacted yet. He waved his arms wildly at Geoff's retreating form.

Okay, out the portal.
Then, in the portal, through the coffee shop.

Without hesitating any further he jumped into the void and onto the hill. The sun was low on the horizon throwing up beautiful silhouettes. Geoff heard a dull thrumming sound. As he prepared to throw the cage back through the portal, he heard loud American voices. One of them he recognized as Jennings. He instinctively ducked down onto the dusty ground.

As he heard a man shouting orders, Geoff cringed and waited to be discovered. The sound of tramping boots ran passed him and went down the hill another way. Geoff looked up and no one was there. As he walked up the hill, cage in hand, Geoff saw where the thrumming sound was coming from and gasped. A giant herd of monstrous animals was heading towards the hill. As he walked upwards, he was able to see more and more. There was a group of men running from the beasts and a group of men running towards the beasts.

He dropped the cage in wonder. Blue made a muffled sound as it landed. Geoff looked down for a moment then looked back at the scene unfolding in front of him.

What happened here? I've only been gone three hours.

18
ENCOUNTER

Ninety Minutes Earlier

Major Clegg tested his breathing apparatus one more time, cautiously making sure the air pressure was consistent and acceptable. Around him half of his squad stood waiting in the classroom eager to head out. They were dressed in ALICE mesh gear, complete with the MOPP Level Four Gear. The Major loved acronyms; they hinted at complex terminology ordinary citizens could not possibly understand. He himself did not know what they meant but he was sure this was the absolute correct gear. The mask was a full wraparound plastic affair that covered his head like a large, stiff balloon. It was attached to the rest of his over suit and was designed to prevent poisonous gases from killing him, and possibly his men as well. The suit made holding things harder and the mask restricted vision but the Major was not going to take any chances with his boys. He had them wearing thick charcoal gloves and Dover boots. They would just have to hold their guns that much tighter, run that much harder, see their targets that much better.

The other half were under strict instructions to stop anyone getting into the academy. His exact instructions had been to 'hold the line'. He figured nine men should be able to stop some teachers from getting into the area. Clegg did not want his younger soldiers to forget their training if they ran into an angry parent, so he had taken all the ammunition from his second team. He also left behind the radio unit. It did not fit over the MOPP uniform. It looked like it had not been used since the Korean War, or rather, the part of that war where America had fought instead of protected.

Blue had been left in his holding pen. The alien had been most uncooperative. The Major had spent a full two hours interrogating the beast with no success. He concluded the animal was merely that; a pet the Englishman had stolen from the alien planet

It was only then Clegg noticed Jennings did not have his helmet cover on.
"Private, why is your mask not on?" he demanded of the tall and altogether far too handsome Private. Major Clegg did not have it in him to trust a man that was better looking than himself. Jennings had the decency to cough and make a face. Clegg was sure if he could have, the Private would have shuffled his feet.

"Sir," the private said, staring ahead impassively, "Myself, Private Baldwin and Private Hennessy have already been in the atmosphere and have suffered no ill effect. Miss Henson and Mr. Nissen have been there on multiple occasions. I am not sure if it's necessary."

"Private Jennings, where did you receive your education on alien planets? We would all love to hear what your doctorate was on? Alien life forms? Alien atmospheres? How far does your knowledge of alien life extend? Perhaps you have a particular insight into their financial systems? The modes of transport? The mating rituals of alien life forms?"

Jennings stared ahead in silence. The Major was known for his style of reprimand. The first section was heavy on sarcasm; the second section was supposedly his reasoning. Jennings had always found his style of 'shock and awe' to be more 'schlock and bore'.

"This planet," continued the Major, "could have affected your body for years to come, Private. I, for one, would like to live long into my dotage. Put on your mask, soldier. We got a planet to investigate."

The Major turned his back on Jennings and moved to the front of the line. He put on his mask, fumbled with the pressure release nervously for a moment and felt the air rush through after a second. Clegg took a moment to straighten his fresh ironed uniform, felt the over suit rub under the feel of his thick gloves, and only then he stepped through. He stumbled down the hill for a second then regained his composure. He paused for a moment, and breathed nervously. Nothing bad had happened. He felt the sweat on his brow already leaking down the side of his helmet cover. He turned around and waved through his men.

The soldiers charged through and ran up the hill. Through Jennings' visor, the sweat droplets formed a fog almost instantly around the edge. Jennings reflected with all the Army equipment at their disposal, the Major really could have made a much better series of choices. ALICE systems had been discontinued for almost a decade in favor of more streamlined, effective systems. The oxygen tank was bulky and heavy. The rifle and the ammunition and the Kevlar and the battle helmet may have been useful if they were entering a war. However, the Major had insisted on only four magazines per soldier which was, in Jennings' considered opinion, insane. It was far less than soldiers carried in war zones. Jennings did not see how all the extra weight was going to help them take samples and investigate. He also did not see how they were properly prepared for a military engagement.

At the hill's summit, the soldiers formed a circle looking out. The Major looked out from the centre of the circle.

"Men," he began, "we have taken the high ground." He beamed at them. This was most important in any engagement as far as he was concerned. The men looked nonplussed. "Split into your teams and complete your objectives. Wilson, take the North quadrant. Hennessy take the East, Jennings the South, and I shall investigate the West." Jennings noticed the Major had chosen the side of the hill with the smoothest gradient as well as the one that offered the greatest view of the portal. Jennings shrugged his shoulders and headed off towards the forest. At least he and his team would be out of sight of the Major.

As soon as they had traveled one hundred metres, Jennings took off his visor, helmet and oxygen tank. His over suit lay in a heap at his feet and he stretched out, smiling as his bones cracked. His team of two stared at him as Jennings took a deep breath of air. He looked over at them. "You looking to live into your dotage?" he said. They looked at each other and then took off their helmets and visors. Soon their entire MOPP chemical suits lay next to the helmets. Jennings undid his jacket and wore it loosely, letting it blow in the soft wind. A large pile of heavy equipment lay in the sun and the three of them stood there, just breathing in the air and stretching. Jennings smiled to himself.

On the other side of the hill, Major Kim led his men sweating and puffing down the hill. It was a surprisingly long march but the hill flattened out onto a large plain. Kim looked out with his binoculars, the only ones the platoon had, and saw a large herd of animals in the distance. They were chewing at the ground. He turned back to his men and pointed at the herd.

"Men, we are going to look at these aliens."

"Sir, that looks like it is quite far."

"Afraid of a walk, soldier?"

"Afraid of running out of oxygen, sir. Also, worried three of us may get eaten."

"Those animals are herbivores. They aren't going to worry about us. They just want to eat grass and not be eaten. Hopefully that will help you breathe easier." The major smiled at the soldier but was not sure if it could be seen. He was finding it a little hard to see with these visor/helmet combinations. He was surprised. Yes, he had been given the equipment the higher ups based at Camp Walker had deigned to send him. He could not believe that a fellow soldier would have deliberately hamstrung another. He plodded ahead and kept his gaze on the dusty ground ahead of him. He took pleasure knowing however hard the going got, that bastard Jennings would be suffering more.

Jennings and his team had collected soil samples and taken pictures of the foliage with his smartphone. That had taken all of five minutes. They were supposed to do this for three hours before meeting again at the summit. Jennings had no idea what else they were supposed to do. None of them were scientists and none had been instructed by a scientist. He looked at his two compatriots, then looked at his watch.

"We got another three hours until we check in. Fancy going for a walk?" They nodded at him and walked into the forest. It was full of gnarly old trees but they were evenly spaced. Aside from the occasional bush, which Jennings was careful to avoid, the going was fairly easy. They had taken a slow circular route, planning to return back to the hill at a different location. Jennings saw a few more birds and took photos. This mission was starting to feel more like a camping trip from his boyhood, although he had not brought rifles on those trips. He smiled to himself. He was fairly sure quite a few of the guys in his platoon definitely brought rifles on their childhood camping trips.

As they made their way through the forest, Jennings wondered if this was the area where the alien they called Blue lived. He thought briefly about Blue and where he was being held and felt a twinge of remorse. He shook it off and focused on the path ahead which opened up into a glade. Just beyond that, the hill was once more present in the background. However, it was not that which grabbed his attention.

In the corner of the glade, there lay a corpse of a giant beast. The other soldiers immediately went into high alert, pointing and waving their guns all around them. Jennings looked at them and rolled his eyes. He ignored the Dynamic Duo and started to take photos of the carcass. It didn't smell that bad; clearly it hadn't been dead that long. Jennings noted the sharp teeth and fearsome claws carefully. This was a carnivore and quite a deadly one at that. Whatever had killed it must have also been quite lethal.

He looked down at the ground. He frowned. There, in the dust, was a shoe print. It was not from the military issue over boots the soldiers were all wearing. He took a photo of it. He noticed more shoe prints of different sizes and took photos of them as well. He then felt the hide cautiously, ready to spring back if the animal was somehow just playing dead. As he traced the smooth white hide along its back up to its red mane he noticed the two holes, one at the base of its neck and one at the base of its head. They were unmistakably bullet holes. He took photos of the holes then looked up at his men.

"Guys, we should get back to the summit and liaise with the Major. He is going to want to know about this." They shouldered their rifles and walked up the steep hill, grabbing hold of tree roots to help their ascent. When they arrived at the top, one of his team tapped him on the shoulder.

"Uh, shouldn't we get the rest of our equipment?" Jennings looked at the young man. He smiled at the gawkish, acne-riddled face. These boys did not deserve to get in trouble over missing equipment, no matter how useless it was. He nodded his assent and the boys climbed down the hill, leaving Jennings alone.

He looked around the hill. The major could not be seen at first. Then Jennings looked further out and saw the trio of soldiers led by the Major. He swore. It looked like the Major had approached a large herd of animals and had almost completed this endeavor. From the looks of things, the animals were much bigger than the soldiers.

Jennings muttered to himself. "Is he really going to just walk up to those animals? Is he really that stupid?" Jennings stood still for a moment, thinking hard. He came to a decision and jumped back in the portal. He needed to make a call.

On the Eastern ridge, Private Hennessy, Private Semchuk and Private White walked one kilometer from the rendezvous. When they were out of sight of the other teams, Hennessy threw down his helmet and threw himself down next to it.

White frowned. "Er , what do you think you're doing? We have to find samples."

Hennessy looked up at him patronisingly. He pulled out a test tube and dragged it through the dust, filling the tube. He stoppered the tube, put it in his pocket and lay back on the ground. Semchuk sat down next to him and looked up at White.

"Come on, man. Look around. This is a joke. They'll send real scientists later. What the hell are we even doing here?"

White looked down on the others for a moment before grunting his assent. As he unshouldered his pack, he reflected it had been a busy 24 hours and he deserved a break. The three sat against the slight start of the slope and drank their water.

On the Western ridge, Wilson, Levinson and Hanekom stared dubiously at the pretty stream flowing in front of them.

Levinson shook his head. "I'm not going in there. I'm just not."

"It's just water," remonstrated Wilson. The wiry Jew looked at him.

"No, it's not. You don't know that. That could be anything. That could be acid, or ...." Levinson went quiet. On his list of dangerous liquids, acid was right at the top. As far as he was concerned, there did not need to be an 'or'.

The other soldier, Hanekom, pointed at a small, dark brown fish flitting in the water. The Afrikaner accent was still strong, even though he had moved to the States years ago.

"We should get that." Hanekom looked at the other two soldiers who kept looking into the river. He sighed. "Give me the poetjkie. I'll get the damn thing." He grabbed the bucket and stepped into the water.

Hanekom grimaced. As he had made that final step, a series of thoughts ran through his head. One, acid would burn any animal. Two, this animal is fine. Three, it cannot be acid. Four, this is definitely not Earth. Five, alien planets may have completely different rules. Six, this could absolutely be an animal that needs acid to live. Seven, I am definitely not being paid enough.

The large, blonde soldier winced as he stepped into the stream. A brief moment of silence as all present considered the role they had to play in

109

this possible disaster. Nothing happened and Hanekom turned to the other two and shrugged his shoulders.

"Coming in?"

The East ridge was more than idyllic. It was ideal for Hennessy's purposes. It was hidden from the asshat of a Major, it was comfortable to the extent Semchuk had already fallen asleep, and, perhaps most importantly, it had a flat field in front of it. There was no way any aliens could get the drop on them. They would be seen kilometers before they approached the trio. Hennessy looked over to White who was still gripping his rifle and staring outwards ferociously.

"If he wants to stand guard, I am not going to stop him," thought Hennessy, and rolled over. As he napped, his hand dropped onto the still form of Semchuk. It felt incredibly cloying and heavy in the suit. Hennessy and Semchuk were asleep in moments, a spooning of plastic proportions.

Major Clegg stopped walking finally and stood there, hand on his hips, struggling to appear as if he was breathing easily. The visor had maintained a limited field of vision, surrounded by the fog droplets as his head continued to sweat under the red sun. The boots had become heavier with every step and the Major had had to fight off a panic attack from being so constricted in the suit. Despite his current sweaty state of fatigue, the Major was suddenly elated. He had walked somewhere no one had ever been before and in front of him, not more than forty meters away, stood the most impressive creature he had ever seen.

The behemoth was larger than a big rig and was covered in blue gray scales. It resembled a giant fish, with its drooping mouth sucking at the dust in its path. Large whiskers above and below its mouth formed a brush to help kick up the dust. As the Major watched, large gills pushed out a large puff of dust from the creature. Along its spine was a series of fanned spikes that glistened in the sun. The creature had thick treetrunk legs with a long tapering tail that fell to the floor and dragged behind

110

it. The creature paid no attention to the Major or his subordinates.

"There, do you see? They just eat grass, or whatever passes for it on this godforsaken planet. They pose zero threat to us." The Major felt he was coming from a place of knowledge. After all, his aunt had owned a dairy farm which he had visited during his halcyon youth. He recalled the docile cows and how they were always happy to lick his hand when he sat by the fence. He decided he was going to approach the ....

"Hmmm," thought the Major, "I suppose I must name you. After all, I did discover you." He turned to the other soldiers. "Men, I give you Clegg Rex." Finally, his family and, of course incidentally, he as well, would have a legacy. His men looked unconvinced.

"Clegg Rex, sir? The dog of Clegg?"

"The dog? No! The King of Clegg!"

"They look more like giant land cat fish." Major Clegg turned around and gave the offending soldier a withering glance.

"Stick to the soldiering, boy, I'll be coming up with the names around here." In his head he had already reduced them to Clegg Juniors. They were his babies after all.

Wilson, Levinson and Hanekom had placed themselves in the middle of the stream. Despite the apparent non-acidity of the situation, Levinson was not taking off his pair of sterile gloves. As the others continued to toil, trying to catch fish and tearing up weeds, Levinson leaned back, stretching himself.

That's when he saw the figure. A silhouette, really just a tiny glimmer of movement in the extreme far distance. It was stood still in the larger silhouette shadow of the towers. If the towers were forty klicks away, this creature was at least thirty. Yet Levinson clearly saw him. As he looked on, the sounds of his comrades became muted, the slick ground of the river became as nothing. He felt his eyes being dragged across the plains, zooming along, pulled inexorably. He found himself face to face, yet miles apart from, an imperious figure carved from shadow.

"You're new," someone said. Levinson was not sure if it was him or the creature. In fact, he was not sure if he was anything anymore.

"Drink." Levinson looked down at the stream and calmly ran his gloved hand through the water and let it pass his lips.

White looked outwards. Semchuk and Hennessy had fallen asleep and were currently spooning. After taking a couple of pics on his smartphone, White decided to leave them to it. None of his business. He looked out to the plains. In fact, he shouldn't really interfere at all. It would be downright embarrassing if they woke up and he was there. He should leave. He felt the urge to move away from the sleeping duo. He took a step away. That single step felt so right. He took another, then another. Before he really thought about it, Private White found himself a hundred paces from his original position. That's when he decided he did not need his rifle.

As Major Clegg faced the herd, he saw one of the larger Juniors had faced him. Its tail swished about from side to side and the whiskers had splayed outwards from its mouth, revealing a mouth that was more like a beak. A large lowing sound emitted from the beast. The two soldiers took a step back. The Major was unmoved and unimpressed. The silly cow thought to intimidate a man who had personally stood against the Northern menace for over a decade? He unshouldered his rifle and clicked the safety off.

"A couple of warning shots should remind Junior who's top dog," thought the slight man smugly.

The shots rang out across the plain for miles. Everyone stopped what they were doing and looked around. The two soldiers who Jennings had left scrambled up the hill, worried they were missing out on some action. Hennessy and Semchuk woke up immediately, grabbing their gear almost subconsciously before running up the hill. White shook his head and took stock of his situation. He turned back to join his compatriots. It would take him a while since he had taken off most of his clothes and he had no idea where his rifle was. Thankfully the other two had scrambled up the hill without noticing his current state. Wilson and Hanekom shouted at Levinson. Levinson slowly turned to the others and smiled.

"Let's go," he said and grabbed his gear.

All of the soldiers were suddenly aware of just how stretched they were and more than one commented on the way their walkie-talkies had ceased working as they had entered the breach.

Major Clegg nodded to himself as his warning was heeded by the herd. They ran away in ones and twos before the whole herd was moving away. They moved at a remarkable speed, considering their size. "It was a shame," reflected the Major. "It would have been better to take a few photos before they left." He was sure they would regroup and settle in a little while. The dust kicked up by the monstrous herd was terrific and it formed a large dustcloud making the animals' escape impossible to detect. He ambled back to his men.

"Dumb animals didn't know any better," he said conversationally, setting his rifle back on his shoulder and starting the walk back to the rendez-vous. It had been a good first contact and initial reconnoiter. He was sure the higher-ups would be happy with his report.

Jennings had just begun his communique to the base at Camp Walker when he heard the shots through the portal. The distance of the report did not change the urgency of the situation and relayed "shots fired!" to the receiving station. He grabbed his rifle off the school desk where he had laid it down only minutes before and rushed back through the portal. He hoped whoever it was at the other end of the line had reported it to the relevant officer. Major Clegg had been a liability from the outset and if this had gone FUBAR he was fine with getting in trouble for breaching the chain of command.

As he popped back into the planet's surface he saw his men standing

113

and looking East with slack jawed expressions. He looked where they were looking and grimaced. The trio from the East were heading back but were still a good couple of kilometers away. The dust cloud kicked up by the herd showed that it was traveling away from the trio. As he watched however, the herd wheeled around slowly until it was heading directly back to the Major. He grabbed the emergency flare from his pack, ignoring the gasps from the other two men. He set it off and the red smoke began to pour out, sending a smoke cloud out over the hill. Everyone would hopefully see it and know to come back to the lookout.

"If they'd heard those shots, they should be heading back already," he thought grimly.

Major Clegg saw the red flare on the hill and curled his lip in disgust. It was probably that idiot Jennings freaking out over the gunshots. The nervous fool must be panicking over nothing. When he got to the hill he would have that man sent to a stockade. He looked back over his shoulder and his eyes widened. The herd seemed to be returning to its original spot. The movement coming towards him was impressive enough to make him start to run. He slowed himself down and marched with a bit more of a spring in his step. It would not do to show his men any fear.

"Double time, gentlemen," he clipped to his men and set off to the hill. The herd sounded a lot closer than it had been only a minute before.

Jennings watched from the top of the hill. The other six men had now joined his trio and they waited, watching in grim fascination. The herd was catching up to the Major's trio very quickly. It was clear they would be overrun before they made it to the summit.

"What do we do, Jennings?" murmured Wilson. Jennings looked at the group. All of them looked to him for guidance. Jennings suddenly felt helpless. It was easy to see officers make bad decisions and in those circumstances Jennings could always find better alternative. With no one else giving orders, there was a mantle of responsibility that had suddenly fallen on him and he suddenly was wracked with indecision.

He shook his head at Wilson. "I have no idea." Wilson stared at him for a moment. He and his team had also taken off their visors and air tanks.

114

Wilson straightened himself. "Hennessy, lead your men down to the foot of the hill. Wait for the Major and help them get them up here. Fire on the lead animals. Hopefully they'll break off." Hennessy led his trio down. Jennings stared. Wilson looked hard at him. "Easy to snipe from the back, man. Sometimes, you got to lead your men. You coming with me?"

"Do you think our bullets will stop those things? You're just going to piss them off!" Jennings retorted. Wilson shook his head and pointed at Jennings.

"Our Major is in trouble. We need to go help him. Unless you got a better idea." Jennings didn't and was amazed that when everyone else started moving down the smooth incline, his legs responded and he found himself running alongside the others. They made it to the bottom of the hill. Suddenly, Jennings saw that they had utterly compromised their position. They had sacrificed the higher ground and better field of firing for only a few hundred yards. He looked back to the summit and saw the danger in which all the men had placed themselves.

The herd's stampede was so loud it threatened to burst the Major's eardrums. The double time had been replaced by straight out sprinting. His two men had left him behind and his visor was leaving him gasping for breath. He saw his soldiers running down the hill, too slowly. They waited for him. He was only a few hundred meters from them. He dared not looked back but he was sure the Juniors were only seconds behind him. He turned and fired wildly into the herd. Within seconds his clip ran dry, and he ran on, trying to put another clip in. Focused on the action, he stumbled on a rock and fell.

Jennings saw the Major go down, only a football field's length away from them. The herd was still a kilometer away but it was moving swiftly.

"He is absolutely going to die," thought the private. "And we're next." Idly, he looked at his watch. It was only 9:30.

19
COLLISION

"Freeze! Put your hands up!" The shouted command had its intended effect. Geoff shot his hands up and stood ramrod stiff, sill facing the oncoming herd. "Turn around slowly and pick up the cage. Bring it back through the portal and I'll do my damnedest to not shoot you in all sorts of places."

The line should have been much better.
I can hear your fear.
Of course I can smell my fear because there's a gun being pointed at my back.

Geoff did not turn around. He winced as he spoke.
"I think you should know your Major and the other men are about to die," he began. The snicker of a gun being cocked silenced him.

"Don't you goddamn threaten me!"

"I'm not. But you should come and see this."

"See what?"

You aren't even on this planet.

116

For him to be able to point a gun at the teacher's head and yet not see the increasing danger in the vicinity, he would have to be limited by the wall of the classroom. Geoff pointed ahead of him, which was to the soldier's right.

"There. All your soldier friends. They are about to get trampled. They need your help."

The sound of silence.
Probably trying to work out how full of shit I am.
That's fair.

"It's perfectly safe to come out here," continued Geoff. "You don't need a gas mask or anything like that."

"Says you!"

Yes, says the guy breathing in and out and walking and talking and staying alive.
Staying alive.
Although I can see how this could scare the BeeGeesus out of someone.
I hate myself.

"Look, are you going to help your Major or not? He needs you and your friends now. NOW!" The shout had its intended effect.

The sound of a soldier failing to land properly on another planet should have had more swearing.
This silence is downright sheepish.

Geoff dropped his hands and turned around. Looking down the hill he could see the portal and the bruised soldiers all staring either up at him, staring at the world around Geoff, or at the soldier lifting himself off the ground and dusting himself off. The young soldier wore wire-frame glasses through which he now squinted at Geoff.

No wonder he didn't sound a threat.
Be nice to the tiny boy with the big gun.

117

"First step is not a big one," said Geoff kindly. The soldier smiled.

"Yeah, got confused about, you know, planets and stuff," the soldier ended his sentence looking down at the toes. The other soldiers grinned at each other.

At least he tried, you pathetic excuses for henchmen.

"Something funny? At least he stepped into the breach. Are you coming to help or are you too busy smirking like idiots. Move, gentlemen!" The other soldiers all jumped through and ran up to the summit to be near Geoff. As they came close to him, the first shots were fired.

Jennings saw how close the lead animal was to the Major and grimaced as he watched his superior take a tumble. Inwardly, he rolled his eyes. Outwardly, he was a solid professional goddamn soldier.

"Covering fire! Short bursts, make them count!" He flicked the safety off and squeezed the trigger.

Major Clegg turned around and looked at the Clegg Rex fill his world. The head loomed over him, almost as if the creature didn't even see the Major, almost as if the Major was not the reason for the stampede, for the naming of its very being.

"Don't you even recognize me?" thought Major Clegg.

The creature's head snapped back and then its body slumped forward. The last thing the Major saw was the gaping fish mouth enveloping him. Teeth and beak fought to grind and chew him before spitting him back out, a mangled corpse. His feet remained in their boots on the ground; bloody stumps the only visual clue the Major had been standing there a second before.

The Major disappeared from view and more of the creatures roiled past. The other two soldiers had made it back to the platoon, wheezing and sobbing. Jennings shook his head. Apparently Shock and Awe would need a lot more heavy artillery than they were able to offer. He eyed the distance between them and the creatures.

"Fall back!" He got up and shouldered his weapon. "Fall back to the portal!" As he ran, he saw a silhouette of a man on the hill. Was the man waving? As he watched, the silhouette was joined by more men. Jennings whooped as he recognised the rest of his troupe. He ran easily past most of his men. He ran alongside Wilson.

"Looks like the calvary has arrived," he grinned to Wilson. Wilson merely grunted and redoubled his efforts. Jennings joined him. His group had made it to the foot of the hill. The troupe at the top of the hill ran down to meet them. Jennings swore. They were going to make the exact same mistake he and Wilson had just made. He waved his hands at them, stopped, pointed furiously at the creatures and then pointed at the men on the hill.

"Shoot them!" He screamed. The men as one hoisted their weapons and took aim. They fired at the animals. Jennings and the others closest to him fell to the ground as the hail of bullets sounded out. Thirty seconds later, it was all over. Jennings looked up. At the top of the hill from his low angle, the men looked strangely far away. One of them cupped his hands around his mouth and shouted down.

"Out of bullets! Run!!"

And that was when the first animal ran past Jennings. As he turned to look at it run past in what seemed like slow motion, he saw one of the Dumb and Dumber twins get hit by the creature's foreleg. The private flew up for a second before falling under the same creature's tail. Jennings reached out for him and felt himself being pushed over. AS he turned to face his own fate, he saw it was not a creature but Wilson who had grabbed him and moved him .

"We need to go. NOW!" said WIlson and then he was gone. His arm still gripped Jennings' shoulder but the rest of him was borne upwards by one of the creatures. As he turned, he seemed untouched by the creatures yet his platoon were stomped on or torn to shreds. He stood, dumbfounded, paralysed, as he somehow stayed in the eye of the bloody maelstrom surrounding him. A streak of electric blue filled up one side

119

of his vision. As he turned to look, it was replaced by a different scene. And that was when he noticed the street filled with cars right by him.

20
ENDGAME

Anne walked away from Geoff and swore quietly under her breath as she went down the stairs. Her friend did not look in the mood to leave town, despite her warning. That would make things messy down the line. She pulled her phone out and sent two texts to different people, both of whom knew nothing of the other. One was General Stevens at Camp Walker, the head of the American forces in this part of Korea. The other man was Moon Jay Min, or as he preferred, Jamie Moon. Jamie Moon was a local councilor. More importantly, he was her Korean liaison with The Company. Both were powerful men, both owed her favors and both needed to be apprised of the current situation.

Major Clegg had been an embarrassment but was a necessary failure. Running him down from the Border had allowed brighter, younger, cooler heads to slot into that position. She had chosen him to run a simple recon mission, to locate and make official its existence. She had then planned to repudiate his claims, and mask its presence to the political divisions in Washington until such time as The Company was able to use it to their advantage. Having been given this assignment to screw up on a temporary basis, the Major would presumably have been given the desk job in Washington the Army so badly needed him to have. However, the Major had gone completely off the rails. He had managed to take a basic reconnoitre and turned it into a diplomatic clusterfuck. The Major needed to be relieved.

General Stevens had been openly critical of Major Clegg, and was eager to help in whatever way necessary to remove the offending officer. He had known of Anne's plan and had therefore supplied Clegg with the least functional equipment. He had been worried at the time the Major would somehow turn out to have hidden depths of excellence. That had not come to pass. When Stevens received the text, he could hardly contain the glee in his voice.

"It's go time," he muttered and buzzed his secretary. He ordered an emergency meeting of his top officers. Anne knew that by sundown, the American Army would have the entire block surrounded.

Jamie Moon was a smart, soft spoken man who was known to think first and act later. Having worked his way up the bureaucratic ladder through a combination of family connections and a pragmatic approach to red tape, Anne needed his type more now than ever. When Anne wanted changes to occur quickly, she had learned local government members were both more capable and more available to effecting that change. If the calculations she had made on the portal were to be believed, the whole city block could be compromised in only a matter of weeks.

Not that it would matter, she considered as she got into a cab. As soon as a news outlet had a video of the portal it would be almost impossible to cover up. Luckily these days, the Internet provided ample opportunity for media chaff and flare. Enough Photoshopped portals around the world would make this real one hopefully quite unbelievable. However, in the meantime, she needed Jamie Moon to close down the streets around the block and run alternate traffic routes for a while.

Jamie Moon looked at Anne's text in annoyance. He had a hundred other issues affecting his city that needed more urgent attention. If any other *weigookin* had dared to text him at all, let alone in such a preemptory manner, it would have been ignored. However, Ms. Henson had proven a very useful contact. In fact, were he given to dark introspection, he could conclude she was not a person he should cross, considering the nature of their previous business. He sighed, then made a phone call. In a short while, that section of the city would be in a traffic nightmare. He hoped it was worth it.

Anne's cab stopped outside the warehouse. She naturally knew the Major's base location, having been the one to establish it. She only hoped the soldiers she had assigned to him were with him at the school. Choosing the youngest, most inexperienced soldiers, or the ones with the worst records to work under the Major had been the smart move, since it meant the highest chance of failure. However, she had felt bad knowing their records were going to be ruined. There was almost no chance any of them were going to be anything but dishonorably discharged.

She unlocked the door and walked in. She took a moment to listen for any movement. Silence filled the warehouse. She moved quickly and quietly to the holding room. The alien designate Blue had been sent here under orders. The Major never knew that she was behind the orders, behind all his orders. Opening the holding room, she looked inside and sighed. It was empty.

"You had one job to do, Clegg, one job!" she shouted.

Where there should have been a cage to hold the alien, there was a bunch of nothing. Anne balled up her fists, fighting the urge to continue ranting. The Major had only one thing she wanted him to do correctly and he had absolutely failed. Only this time, his failure could have cost her as well.

21
BLUE

He had been a part of the government, working as a Law Officer outside the city. He had been mocked by those whose whole life existed within its gleaming spires. They did not really consider those who chose life in the rolling plains to be worthy. He had been happy, important to make a difference and respected amongst those with whom he dwelled.

The city dwellers had other thoughts. When they had become bored and looked for entertainment, it had been his extreme bad luck to be within the city limits. They had hunted him down, chasing him through the alleyways and sewer tunnels. They laughed at his attempts to hide from them. The laughter still haunted him. No one could hide as well as him but no one could hunt as well as them.

He was caught and placed within the Control chamber, fixed upon a twitted crucifix, made of shadow and blood. When they performed their machinations, the last sound he had uttered had been a scream of agony. When he awoke, he had been stripped naked, banished from the city and could never utter another sound.

He had returned to his community only to find the banishment had extended to there as well. Unable to meet his eyes, they had sent him on. He left, bloody footprints the only sign he had ever been there at all. In time, the dusty wind had removed even those.

Life had been brutal. Slowly he had become more and more feral, until the thought of cooking the birds he ate became a far thought. He lived in a tree and slowly he became the joke they said of him in the City; a Beast pretending to be more.

Time passed.

A hole appeared. It was like the hole in his tree but in the very air by his jumping branch. He discovered it quite by chance. Launching himself off as he had done so many times before, to catch birds in flight, on this occasion he missed the bird and fell into somewhere .... Else.

A man was speaking to children. An actual man! He was flesh and blood and walking and talking and the legends were real!

The man used words he recognized. In a flood, his brain's subconscious ripped away the walls and safeguards put up. The degradation he had suffered for years, the torment his people had gone through, the torture leading to his mute state. He couldn't take it. He ran away, back to his tree. He hardly noticed the paint on his feet.

He cried, soundlessly, alone.

He returned, drying his eyes and determined to make a good impression. A human! Truly remarkable. Remarkable. He savoured every recollected word as it reentered his consciousness.

He smiled. He high fived. He pointed with both hands, just like the human.

When he saw the man argue with another man, he felt confusion. Who was the leader? Then, he saw the second man curl up in shame and walk away. He felt glee. His first choice had defended his territory. Clearly, this was the Alpha.

When he touched the human for the first time, he was afraid of the mental backlash. Humans were mythical geniuses. Stories abounded of their mental acuity, of their telepathic mastery. When nothing happened, he stared at the human. Maybe they had taken that from him too. A final

125

ignominy he had been spared until now. Blue turned away, prepared to be alone forever.

He returned when he heard shouting. Jumping through the portal was easier now. The hole had become bigger every time he touched it. One time he saw a bird had flown through and he widened the space so he could kill and eat it. The human had made it increasingly clear he wanted to communicate. His name was Geoff. Geoff even let him travel around the Humans' world. He met Geoff's friend, who also really, really wanted to communicate. Her name was Anne. He was glad a female could be near him. The Others had nearly driven that from him.

Then, he had shown them his world.

For a moment, everything was perfect. He had friends. He had a life. He had a soul once again. The humans had fixed him. Or, maybe the Humans had allowed him to fix himself. It didn't matter. He was happy.

Then, everything had gone wrong and he had been thrown into another cage, uncertain of his fate once again. He thought of Geoff and missed his ...friend. He filled his mind with memories of being with him. He felt him somewhere in the cosmos. One time, his friend had become so angry, the wall of consciousness had knocked Blue over. He asked his friend to stop, and he had.

Kindness.

He knew his friend was looking for him and he made him feel calm. Another time, he felt Geoff and was able to feel himself in his Human mind. Connection had been achieved for the first time in a long time. He looked up at his friend and smiled.

When they landed back on his planet, he saw little from in his cage. When Geoff dropped the cage, the door sprang open and out he popped. Geoff commanded those people he had considered his captors and they obeyed. Truly an Alpha. He watched them run off to protect other humans, only to see them run headlong into a Skrimma herd.

He knew what he had to do. Geoff wanted to save those men. Geoff was Blue's friend. Blue would save them.

Blue ran to his tree and climbed his climbing branch. He ran along it and jumped at the portal. However, he mistimed and angled his jump. He hit the side of the portal and held on. As he fell down, the hill fell away with him, his fall becoming an extended zipline between worlds. He held onto the portal.

It widened tremendously. Blue flew past the hill to where the soldiers were facing the Skrimma. He held onto the portal.

The rift stretched and exploded out, becoming a long expanse of ripped sky, bordered by the mystical energy. Finally he landed on the ground.

22
STAMPEDE

Mr. Kim stayed huddled in the doorway of his local GS25, trying to smoke a thin cigarette and cry. This particular convenience store had been the site of many of Mr. Kim's lonely drinking sessions, so the owner knew better than to bother the school director. His entire livelihood, his entire life had just been ripped out from him. Americans, and that *keseki* of an Englishman, had destroyed him.

He looked down the avenue. He could see his tower at the end of the block. If he squinted his eyes he could just make out the tiny poster flag that still flew over the school. His school. His school that was now closed and his reputation tarnished. Combined with his low level of qualification and inability to follow instruction, owning an English *hagwan* seemed like the only way he would ever make money, and now even that was gone.

He wondered what he was going to do next. He looked around the crossroads and wondered if anyone else knew he was unemployed. He wondered how many of his students' parents had told their friends. He contemplated running out into the traffic. He laughed to himself. In the current situation, no one would be running him over. Traffic stuttered and stopped through pouring rain.

"G-d, please send me a sign as what to do." He thought the prayer as hard as he could, willing the message to be flung into the ear of He who could affect a change.

Suddenly a melted landscape appeared. It slid out from the window of his floor of the tower. It was a rip in his reality and his eyes bugged out at what happened. Where blue gray drizzle had been, there was now a tear of red sunshine. He watched as it descended overhead. The view of towers in the distance, half hidden by misty, polluted rain, was replaced by a clear impossibly red sky, by rolling plains, by a massive hill that descended to the crossroads. The top of the rip stayed at the same height while the bottom of the rip flew diagonally down to ground level. More and more red sky showed.

Mr. Kim's cigarette fell out of his nerveless mouth. He heard screaming and saw an alumna dropped her shopping at the site. The first cars crashed. Drivers moved sideways to stop themselves going into that vista and to avoid hitting the cars on either side of them.
Traffic, already a slow beast at this time of day, stopped and died.

The aberration stretched all the way to the ground and continued until it crossed the ten lane street. Mr. Kim looked across the massive intersection. Cars drove sideways, frantic to get away from the sight. Red sun rays created sunset shadows. Mr. Kim slowly stood up and swallowed nervously. Now he could not see the cars on the other side at all.

Instead, he saw a herd of animals approaching at incredible speed. They were huge and grotesque. They looked like the stuff of nightmares, and Mr. Kim stepped down into the street to see them better. There was a large dust cloud forming behind them. They seemed to be heading up the hill.

More cars crashed. The noise of screeching metal could be heard clearly even from Mr. Kim's position. Two petrol tankers blared their horns angrily as they found their way across the intersection blocked by screaming *ajummas*. The drivers who should have been waiting for the light to go green were not. With cars blocking their desperate reverse exit strategy, cars simply rammed into each other until no one could maneuver. A sickly mishmash of cars folded into each other. Those men and women lucky enough to not be hemmed into their vehicles by the surrounding traffic bolted out of their cars and dove for cover.

The creatures heard the horns and turned their spiny, whiskered heads towards the sounds. As they ran, they followed the offering of an easier way to stampede -- away from the red hill and towards the traffic. Towards Mr. Kim.

The herd ran through the rip.

They touched down on the concrete and seemed enraged by the change in terrain. They moved effortlessly, through and over the cars, stomping them flat or sending them into the sky. Mr. Kim watched as one woman was trapped in her car and squashed by one of the gigantic legs. He watched as one car appeared suddenly from behind the rift. It crossed the portal line as it drove forward and a Skrimma paw stepping through merged at the same time. The Skrimma pierced through the vehicle and the front half of the car was flung forward, its owners screaming at it landed in a heap.

The two petrol tankers were hit on their sides and thrown through the air. The first tanker slammed into the school tower, flying into the bank on the first floor and disappearing from the director's view. The second leaned against the corner of his building. Inside the bank, a quiet morning was destroyed in a nanosecond. The tanker flew through the windows, causing the old security guard to dive out of the way. Customers screamed and squealed as the tanker slid into and over them. It came to a rest as the cab faced the cashier. She had the brief pleasure of a moment of silence as she stared at the groggy driver and the array of fluorescent Miss Kitty's lined along his dashboard. Then the tanker exploded. The cab was shot forward into the cashier, crushing her and the desk. The Hello Kitty's and the heavy engine flew into one the main support beams, causing the whole structure to groan ominously. The survivors peered out from the chaotic debris spread around the bank.

Mr. Kim had been lifted off his feet as the blast had filled the air. Both tanker explosions inside the bank had blown out the glass windows before sending out a loud creaking screech. Mr. Kim got back up to his feet quickly. The blast had launched the cars nearest the building clear across the street. A few of the animals had been pushed down by the blast but they got up and joined the rest of the herd as they ran down the street. The buildings on the other side of the road had also become so much shattered glass. The flames from the tanker wrapped around the corner of Mr. Kim's building, with black smoke and bright flames pouring up the side of the wall.

Panic filled the air. People ran for tower entrances, only to be gored by the creatures. Mr. Kim dove into the GS25 and hid behind the fridge. The animal's thunderous approach became a terrifying avalanche of sound. Mr. Kim hugged his knees. The owner had hidden behind his counter. Then, in what seemed like only moments, it was replaced by a dearth of movement.

Mr. Kim opened his eyes and looked cautiously out from his hiding place. The doorway seemed quiet. He got to his feet and walked carefully out along the street. The monsters had gone. Only the sounds of car alarms, mourning their suffering, and those people crying out for help remained. The dustcloud continued down the street. The monsters had gone right up the highway. Buildings, roads, cars, people, none had remained untouched. However, the intersection was deserted. The Skrimma had piled through and were heading North.

Mr. Kim looked back to his tower and gritted his teeth. The fire was wildly out of control. As he watched, he heard it give a long, shuddering groan. Mr. Kim thought quickly. His insurance was still valid until the end of the month. In a scene of cataclysmic catastrophe, his tower seemed to be shining gold.

"Thank you, Lord," said the Director. "Thank you for hearing my prayer!"

23
TOWERING

Geoff watched the rift open up in front of him. He gaped as he saw Blue streak off down the hill, and the portal tore the sky. A slit of blue gray split the red sky and the split slowly dragged down to the ground. Through the portal, Geoff could clearly see the traffic for a moment. Then the Skrimma stepped through. As the herd stomped their way in, their bodies touched the sparkling edge of the portal, pushing it further open. Geoff had a perfect view of the carnage that unfolded. Almost all the Skrimma left their original target of the soldiers on the hill and went up the main high street, full of cars, full of the cars' ex-occupants running and screaming. One dazed male driver just stood there and disappeared as the herd moved through. Geoff winced at his grisly fate.

Skrimma. That is absolutely what they are called.
Blue.
Someone's been expanding my vocabulary.

Blue stopped and waved at the English teacher. Geoff waved back then suddenly thought how odd he must look, floating in the Korean sky. He wondered if he should still reenter Earth through his classroom. At this point, he could just walk down the hill and into the high street. The only thing that was stopping him was the band of soldiers who looked quite the worse for wear. He was fairly sure he could saunter past them and into his old life.

One of the last Skrimma in the herd, an old, scarred beast, did not follow his companions. He was one of the largest in the herd, standing almost twice the height of most of the other animals. He took one look at the beeping and alarm sounds, the bright lights of the Korean city and turned his head back towards the hill. Geoff felt the creature's shift in direction and felt a dull ache in the pit of his stomach.

He's coming for me.
So much for that jaunt down the hill.

The Skrimma picked up speed going up the hill, its powerful legs pushing deep into the ground. The soldiers dived out of the way and the Skrimma kept on, undeterred. Geoff backed up slowly, his feet walking as though through tar. The Skrimma let out a piercing squeal, throwing its whiskered beak into the air. It was now only fifty yards away and incredibly still picking up speed. Geoff could sense the animal's rage at the change in his environment, his indignation that someone as Geoff would ruin his life. The Skrimma's beeline shortened the gap even more. Geoff turned and ran for the rift. With one step he was in his classroom and he turned around.

The Skrimma seemed to fill up the classroom view as time slowed to a trickle. Its beak was clearly visible as its whiskers were fully splayed out. As the beak opened, Geoff could see the pulsing red flesh within. The breath of the animal made Geoff want to gag, its noxious odour similar to fish left out in the sun. The front legs stepped through the portal and landed on the floor of the classroom, crushing the military radio.

Geoff knew he was going to die. It was not in dispute. His end would be the same as the old man in the Korean High Street; quick, painful and ignominious. Time slowed as the whisker left a velvet touch across the individual baby hair follicles on his cheek. The beak opened up before Geoff's head, only four feet away. Geoff found he had time to wonder if everyone had this much time in their final moments, if time slowed like this for all people.

Or is this because of Blue?

133

Then, the beak fell down and was stopped short. The Skrimma lay on the floor, its front legs scrabbling for purchase. It back legs had not made the jump through the portal and it squealed in rage once more, being so tantalisingly close to its aggressor, its symbol of annoyance. The back legs scrabbled again. The back legs pushed up into the portal, forcing it down the side of the building. As the portal shot down another twenty feet, the building gave a tearing sound. The floor under the Skrimma's front torso gave way. It fell down and into the cafe beneath Geoff, its back legs crashing through the wall.

The teacher looked down as the creature lay there motionless for a moment. Then it shook its head and looked up at Geoff. He barely had enough time to dive out of the classroom as the Skrimma jumped up on its back legs and snapped at his ankles. As he slid across the dirty vinyl floor, Geoff heard a terrible rending sound.

He turned back and the Skrimma was not there. Cautiously, Geoff crawled back into the room and fearfully looked over the edge of the hole in the floor. He could see the snarling Skrimma writhing in pain as it lay on the floor of the coffee shop. It stared balefully at the baristas. They had taken a moment to look up from their cellphones to witness the unique occurrence. Then the floor groaned and the Skrimma fell through again. It smashed through consecutive floors. Detritus fell with it, and it became part of a swirling dustcloud moving down in a start stop motion. Finally, the Skrimma landed on the ground floor. It burst through the banks' lighting and then lay there, broken fluorescent tubes, wires, masonry and dust all around it. Even from the tenth floor, Geoff could easily hear the screaming of women. Then, incredibly, the Skrimma moved. It stumbled to its feet, turned this way and that before finally lumbering away.

The building let out a dull, ominous moan. Twisted steel beams shrieked their torment. Geoff knew he needed to get out there as soon as possible. The building shifted on its axis and Geoff was flung against a wall. He looked down the corridor and groaned.

The Koreans were still in the hallway.

"Get out of here!" He screamed at them. "The building is going to collapse! Get out! Get out!" Some of them immediately ran down the stairwell. Others instinctively ducked down onto the floor as the building gave another terrifying crumbling sound. One man stumbled to the elevator and pushed the button.

You've got to be kidding me.

He stumbled forward down the corridor and fell against the locked glass door. He flicked it open then fell on the ground with the crowd of teachers and parents. The Koreans stared up at Geoff as they lay strewn against the wall. The man pushing frantically against the lift button looked over his shoulder at Geoff, his eyes wide with fear.

Geoff looked around the room and took a moment. In the current situation, that decision was more than a little brave, yet almost definitely too much stupid. The stairwell presented the best case for a swift exit. As he thought to move towards it, there was a terrible tearing, grinding sound and the whole tower block twisted, first one way, then the other. At once, the stairwell became nothing more than a dust cloud. It imploded on itself, the noise deafening the English teacher. He clapped his hands over his ears far too late. For a moment he fell to his knees and saw stars. He blinked and focused on the fake wooden floor. He observed deeply until the whorls and boles in the flooring became galaxies in his retinas.

Eventually, he managed to stand up and felt someone grabbing his arm. He looked into the concerned eyes of Miss Huang. She was speaking to him but he could only hear a ringing sound. She pulled him to his feet frantically. He looked from her to the others who had gathered around the two teachers.

Another wrenching sound and the wall on the other side of the tower fell away. The wall simply broke apart from the ceiling and floor like cheap shoe parting company with his sole. As it fell away, Geoff was able to see the red sky of Blue's homeworld. Geoff cocked his head and staggered towards the gaping hole. Miss Huang held onto his arm, then his hand as her grip weakened. Standing near the edge, Geoff looked down. At his feet was a mass of torn metal spikes, displaced masonry and, most relevant, a gaping lack of anything directly beneath him. About a meter away the portal pulsed and the red landscape beckoned. The slope of the hill was only a short fall away. Geoff shook his head.

135

Oh well why not?

He grit his teeth. He noticed the coppery taste of blood and realized he had cut his lip at some point. He was suddenly aware of aches and bruises and cuts all over his hands and face. He turned to Miss Huang. She still stood close to him.

"Trust me!" he shouted. Then he threw Miss Huang through the portal.

The Korean woman screamed as she fell backwards. She clawed at the air as she stared at Geoff. Then she landed on the hill and slid along the dirt on her back, before finally rolling up back over her head and lying in the dirt face down. Geoff took a moment to see if she was still breathing. Judging by her moans, Miss Huang was alive although 'shaken' probably would not be the right adjective.

Geoff turned to the group of flabbergasted Koreans.

"Who's next?" he enquired cheerfully. There was a manic glint to his smile. The Koreans slowly shuffled back from him. There was a moment of frozen tableau. Then the building gave another Death Cry and the whole building started to topple towards the intersection.

The man who had been hitting the lift button was completely kitted out in the very latest in survival instincts. He hurtled past Geoff and launched himself out of the now moving hole. The movement was enough to rouse the rest of the group, much like a herd of startled deer. They all ran for the hole and Geoff felt them slide around him. He let them through then ran for the hole as well. The building finally broke free and started to freefall.

Geoff ran in a straight line. As he reached the end of the corridor, he was pushing off the wall as if it was the floor. He hurtled through the portal an saw the dusty ground too far below him. The hill had sloped down considerably by this point and he had traveled a good distance before he slid into its decline. He lay there, feeling the burn against his back and arm. He had definitely lost some skin and his shoulder felt distinctly unimpressed.

136

The booming sound of the building falling next to him, albeit on a different planet, jolted him, and he sat up abruptly on the alien landscape. He looked up along the ridge. Strewn across the hill were the line of Koreans, all complete with their own skid marked entry points furrowed into the ground.

Geoff smiled to himself. He sank back down into the ground, happy to let the aches and pains dictate the pace. Something metallic snickered loudly. It was the unmistakable sound of a gun being cocked. Geoff turned around slowly and looked up into the barrel. Corporal Jennings looked as though he had been through hell. His face was covered in blood. His entire uniform was torn and there were a million cuts on his body. He staggered a moment then stayed still, pointing the gun at Geoff. His eyes and the hands looked dead calm.

"You're coming with me," said the soldier. Geoff nodded, suddenly exhausted.

24
REACTION

Jamie Moon stared at the images coming out of his car's television and swore. Some idiot pilot with a camera had just attempted to breach the no-fly zone. The police had intercepted him, two helicopters from the tactical division sending the budding journalist on his way. Now there was footage of the police choppers to go with endless imagery of police officers armed with riot shields and batons staring impassively at angry residents who had been ousted from their homes.

It didn't matter anyway. The news had hit the Internet almost immediately. YouTube video after YouTube video showed the rift in all its terrifying majesty. The herd of alien beasts had been captured on film at least, if not in reality. Jamie had been informed that they were currently grazing on the banks of the river just outside the city limits. They seemed blissfully unaware of the damage they had caused, as well as the local residents who seemed intent on taking revenge in a culinary manner.

Another alert on his phone from yet another government body. The problem with being known as the local fixer was that everyone wanted you to fix their individual, petty problems. No one seemed to be taking into account the bigger picture of an entire alien planet having been discovered and that its sole contact point was in Daegu, one of the most traditional cities in a traditional country. New ideas took a while to be accepted here at the best of times. Smoking had only just been banned in bars and restaurants. Jamie was sure there would be massive opportunities for Korea because of this, but for the moment he wished the whole thing would just go away.

The car stopped and sighing deeply, Jamie got out. He walked up the steps to the impressive building. It had been chosen ostensibly because it was a government building. Jamie couldn't help noticing it was also in a district located the furthest from the rift. He walked through the corridors to the chosen room and opened the door. All the usual suspects were there; the combination of both public officials who lived off public attention and media adoration and the shadowy figures who controlled the real power in the city. The smoke was thick in the air; clearly none of the men present cared deeply about the new smoking ban. Of course there were no women. Jamie bowed deeply to the table (he had learned the skill of bowing to everyone and to no one all at the same time) and sat down.

Of course all this was just a front. He had gathered together all these people for one reason. The longer the meeting persisted in a room with no reception, and where security had strict instructions not to admit any aides, the more time Anne Henson had to address the situation. Sometimes, doing nothing is the best way to do something.

He wondered what the Americans were doing.

General Stevens stood at his console deck. Beneath him a soldier was readying his drone. Flying from Camp Walker, the small craft would get to the site in only a matter of minutes. The plan was to fly around the site to make sure the keyhole satellite imagery was up to date. The cost of constantly realigning satellites was starting to add up and quite frankly, the General wanted to get a better look at the thing.

He watched the live feed avidly. As he did so, his subalterns would give updates on any changes in the environment data. The General would have been surprised if they had anything untoward to report. Miss Henson had done her work well, and it did not seem as if the alternate planet represented a radioactive or gaseous, or gravitational issue.

And yet, a whole planet was now adjacent to his own. The General did not understand how that was possible. Frankly, he did not get paid to think on the physical ramifications, nor the philosophical implications. All he cared about was the security issue. Already a herd of dumb animals had decimated an urban area of an ally. If this had opened up in New York? The General did not want to think about that. As far as he was concerned, this was the ideal way to deal with a rift opening up to an alien planet. On allied soil, so Americans had unfettered access, yet not damaging Americans or their way of life.

Perfect.

The drone flew around the rift. It came at it from behind so when it first showed on screen, it appeared first as a line in the sky. Then the entire became visible but the view slowly disappeared as the drone turned.

The General grew impatient.

"We need to send it into the rift," he said to the pilot. The pilot started, and then grinned.

"Yes sir!"

The drone flew low around the back of the rift, whizzing over the main street. Below it, Mr. Kim waved at the small aircraft. He had been on a happy drinking session outside the local GS25 since the tower had collapsed. On his plastic table there were five empty bottles. He had danced a jig when he realised he was still alive, and that his failure of an academy was gone, but insured to the maximum. Mr. Kim had never been rich before but he was sure it started with being drunk.

The drone flew around, taking a longer arc so it could line up its trajectory properly. The General and the pilot could now see the entire rift in front of them, covering eight lanes of the thoroughfare.

"Angle is good," the pilot said in clipped, professional tones. He was quite sure the President would be watching this in his War Room. The drone approached the rift at speed. The pilot aimed to the right of the hill, seeking the flat plains promised beyond. He was going to be the first person to see this planet. Sure that English guy had been in here a couple of times, and the GIs had reconnoitered around the hill. However, within a minute he would have recorded a million times more information.

The drone hit the rift.

The drone went through the rift. All the instruments flared and the drone went into a tailspin.

"The drone is not responding," the pilot said. That amazingly, was not the biggest problem.

The drone was still on Earth. As it flew through the line it did not go into the Red Planet. Instead its tailspin sent it flying directly into the path of a convenience store.

Mr. Kim saw the drone craft fly towards him. He watched it not disappear into the rift. Instead it loomed larger and larger as it aimed directly at him. Mr. Kim stared at it then dove into the alleyway next to the convenience store.

The drone flew into the store and smashed into the ice cream freezer cabinet. It blew up, exploding inside the store. The General saw it all happen on the feed.

"Well," he said. "That's not ideal."

"Sir, no sir," said the pilot, his forehead covered in sweat. He wondered if Amazon was hiring.

25
ONE WEEK LATER

Anne sipped her coffee and surveyed the situation. The coffee was much too hot, so she blew on it occasionally to cool it down. Still, she managed to burn her mouth repeatedly on the scalding liquid. She reflected that the coffee and the situation around her had similarities. Both were major problems in her life and it seemed the systems in place to stop the problems were utterly ineffectual.

The junction of the school tower disaster was an apocalyptic nightmare. Twisted metal, the remnants of burned out cars and buses along the avenue showed clearly where the stampede had gone. Cracks in the road showed both the tracks of the beasts, as well as the terrible concrete used by cheap road construction companies. The skyscraper had as yet not cleared away. It was nothing more than a pile of rubble at this point. The dust thrown up by the collapse had got onto and into everything. The first responders were covered in it.

Anne took another sip and looked at the people who had demanded her presence. The Koreans were gesticulating at each other, at the scenery, but mostly at Anne which she did not think was entirely fair. The Americans were very carefully setting up shop in a way that was polite to the Koreans in charge, with a strong and definite finality. The

Koreans had already cordoned off the building. However, the US army had cordoned off the entire block surrounding the tower.

Anne looked up to the skies and sighed. Then again, the biggest bugbear she faced was the number of news helicopters hovering overhead. The one thing she had been instructed was very important was a low profile with no media. Again, Anne felt slightly put upon. She was not the reason the press showed up yesterday and never left.

She looked at the portal's landscape. The border of the tear was one long series of muted blue electric arc. The black of the night was very jarring in the midday sun, even if it was the feeble wintry fare favored by Daegu in March. She briefly wondered what the view was from the other side then shook her head. Thoughts like that were probably dangerous at this time, given the political climate.

The Rift, was how one enterprising helijockey had referred to it. Journalists generally being the kid in class who always copied his neighbour, Anne was not surprised to see the name used by the other alleged investigative journalists. She watched with grim humour as the helicopters made damn sure they never went too near the Rift (dammit, it was a good name).

The military arrest of Geoff had made the news and he was already being castigated, held up as the person responsible for all that happened -- starting with the Rift opening, and ending with the deadly stampede throughout the northern edge of the city. He was being hailed as the new terrorist du jour. *Rolling Stone* were rumored to want an interview. Anne was not quite sure where Geoff was being held. It was not going to be somewhere pleasant. The news was running old footage from the UK, showing a river flooded with pollution. Apparently, he had been involved with that as well. Officially, everything was still under investigation by the proper authorities. Officially, Geoff was being touted as the Most Dangerous Man In The World, a terrorist and an environmental lunatic.

Not even the public testimony of several Koreans who had been trapped in the tower and allegedly rescued by Geoff had not done much to change public perception. The footage of him being put into a black van, manacled on both his feet and hands had made Anne very angry.

Actually, if Anne ever thought about Geoff and all he was being held accountable for, and how it was probably going to end for him, she was liable to crush something.

Mr. Kim had become a media sensation overnight in Korea. As a former owner of a business in the tower, he was charged with being the voice of the Man in the Street. Unrepentantly patriotic and constantly spewing vitriolic diatribe with regards to American Forces and English Dangers, he had gone over well with the Morning Coffee TV brigade. Anne did not doubt he was seeing more money than he had ever seen in his whole life. She heard that one of the K-Pop stars wanted to date him.

Of course, no one had tried to send a single vehicle into the Rift since the drone incident about two days ago, about six hours after Geoff's arrest. The Americans had not sought the Koreans' permission before sending in one of their drones. The drone flew into the Rift, then promptly disappeared. At least, that was what everyone on one side of the Rift saw. On the other side the drone flew through as per usual.

There had been two results from this. One, there was consensus that machinery could not pass through the Rift, hence the helicopters keeping away from the portal. Pilots did not like traveling when their vehicle was likely to stop being around them. Second, the Koreans were making damn sure no one else, including the Americans were going through the Rift. Two armored personnel carriers and a brigade of Korean troops stood impassively in front of the Rift at what had used to be street level.

Anne finished the last of her coffee and threw the cup on the ground. It did not seem to matter so much in the scheme of current affairs. She walked up to the Koreans whose conversation had devolved to a shouting match. She pushed her way into the center of their huddle.

"Gentlemen, you must control yourselves. The press is having a field day; the city needs urgent attention. Korea is looking incompetent and dangerous. It's been one week and where are we? The animals roam free, the helicopters are still flying. Fix this now. Now I know you all understand me, and I know you're not going to argue. Right?" The last word would have been at home in The South Pole. No one dared argue and the diminutive woman took one last look around the circle of old men, then walked on.

The American military were entirely military. Since she had the ear of the General, and he nodded acknowledgement of Anne, she decided to let them be. Her boss was heading out to Daegu. When that happened, Anne had no idea if she would be promoted, or fired, or even noticed. All she knew was that, as she trudged back through the debris away from everyone, she needed another cup of coffee.

26
SOURCE

Kim Ga Bin had not slept properly since she had awoken in the coffee shop one week ago. In that time, her apartment had had a first class view of the Rift. Since it would be daytime when the rest of Korea was having night, the light was constant. Not that it would have mattered anyway. The nightmares she experienced always kept her sleep to what seemed like seconds, before waking to sweats and ragged breathing. She had managed to keep herself from screaming so far, although this last time had been close. She could still feel the bite mark on her hand she performed on herself to keep from waking her parents.

She got out of bed and walked over to her wall-length window. Her father was rich enough to own a high rise apartment right on the corner of the affluent intersection. Normally the mega screens advertising baby formula and soju would not be nearly enough to keep Ga Bin awake. However, this Rift shone directly into her room. It looked peaceful currently, although she knew how dangerous its denizens were. She knew better than most.

She touched her leg and thought hard. The wound was still recovering from where the... thing had slashed at her, had fallen into her. The flesh was a mass of purple and yellow bruising. She thought of the fat American woman who had saved her life, of the English teacher who had helped. This man had been dubbed in the news as The Most

Dangerous Man in The World. She rubbed her leg and shook her head. It just didn't feel right.

Kim Ga Bin got out her notebook and turned on her camera.

"My name is Kim Ga Bin. I have been to the other planet. The Most Dangerous Man in The World saved my life," she began.

27
STABILITY

In the two weeks since the stampede, the general had had to admit the drone incident had been a partial failure. Yes, it had failed to actually enter the Rift. Admittedly, it had lost a little control for a couple of seconds there, maybe even a minute. However, no one had died and it had performed an auto landing quite well. It was a shame the convenience store had been right there but there were too many of the damn things around and hardly anyone had been hurt.

Most importantly, someone pointed out the Rift was a wall, stopping things going through from one side only. Once a transport had driven down the street past the Rift, it could not go back that same way. The General's aide had responded to the unfortunate subordinate snidely, saying how the Rift was not hard to bypass since it was only the size of a large trunk road, and that there were plenty of other roads to use instead. The General thought differently. He had been shown the growth of the Rift in the time period it had been studied. At that current rate, the Rift was going to be much bigger than anyone had currently anticipated. He saw logistics in the future becoming a major problem.

However, two weeks on, the Rift had stabilised and the news crews were getting bored with the absolute lack of activity around it. Jamie Moon was a genius. By removing most of the soldiers, and working with the US government to make their presence less felt, the Rift did not

148

look nearly as forbidding. Of course, a large construction boundary fence had been placed around the entire Rift, and the airspace for five kilometers around the it had been shut down. Effectively, the news crews could only film a giant blue tent.

With no footage, the news networks had been forced to rely upon their talking heads to provide conjecture. Within five days, even the most longwinded gasbags had shut their trap. At that point, new news had been sought after in this drama.

So tonight, the memorial of Major Jarrod Clegg had been a welcome godsend, and the U.S. Army was always happy to have one of their own be treated as a hero. A candlelight vigil had been set up one street beyond the blindside of the Rift. A statue was being commissioned. For now, the images of hundreds of Koreans and Americans holding faux candles as the lament of the Last Post played out over the speaker was compelling video imagery.

The surviving five soldiers from the ill-fated mission, all which remained from a squad of twenty stood on a pedestal, each holding a candle. They looked suitably sad yet capable. All of them retained a haggard look even as their uniform looked pressed to a perfect finish. The General felt sorry for them for a moment then reminded himself they were serving a purpose. Of course there was a sixth. Private Jennings had been sent to the stockade. A man capable of disobeying orders was simply not the right image the Army needed to convey at this point. It was not the first time Jennings had broken the chain of command. Admittedly, his actions had given the General a few minutes head start on his Korean peers but Jennings simply had to go.

The crowd of people held together peacefully. By Korean standards, anything less than a thousand was a small gathering. There was almost no chance of violence on the streets these days, especially with the agents placed among the crowd to locate possible trouble makers and remove them. The General looked once again at the Five. White, Hanekom, Levinson, and Semchuk had been with the Major in the first sortie. Levinson had been a hero by all accounts, calmly walking through the herd of animals to pull Hanekom out of certain doom. The young man with the glasses and nervy disposition, Rodriguez had pulled White and Semchuk out of the Rift after the herd had passed. That little

Mexican may have saved both their lives.

The General made a note to keep track of their movements.

28
RIFT

Anne was watching the broadcast on her phone as she walked through the impressive hallway of the building she called her work. The room was designed to let outside dignitaries know from the outset they were dealing with issues beyond their ken and with people above their knowledge pay grade. Normally, she would take her time in the atrium, wanting those outsiders to see her seeing them. It often saved time later on. However, on this occasion she only had eyes for her cell phone and walked into the elevator.

The ceremony looked to be going well. Jamie Moon and the General had liaised well and followed her 'suggestions' well. Hopefully the media blackout and the headfake with the commemoration ceremony would allow the people upstairs to decide what the next move should be. Anne had a few ideas but she knew how to bide her time until the correct idea met the right moment.

The elevator went up to the fourth floor. As the doors opened, the security guard nodded to her from behind the safety glass. Clearly, the security up here was a show but the men themselves were no joke. Anne nodded back and walked down the corridor before knocking on a door. There was no response. Anne let herself in.

"Morning soldier," said Anne to Private Jennings. The man had not moved since he had returned through the Rift. Compared to his ID photo, Jennings looked like a changed man. His eyes were sunken and his stubble was definitely not Army regulation. She noticed his nails were ragged and still had dirt under them. She wondered idly what planet it was from. She also noticed almost all the cuticles on his right hand had been chewed off. Apparently he had watched as his good friend had been ripped in half in front of him.

"Jennings? I'm hoping you're enjoying our stockade." The General had no idea Jennings had not been taken by Anne, nor that the Private was in line for a commendation. The simple fact was that Private Jennings had shown an aptitude to survive and think on his feet in a truly alien environment. Without his quick thinking there would have been zero survivors. "Take your time, enjoy the amenities. Anything you want, just ask for it." Anne's little half smile and momentary closed eyes provided the rest of that statement. As long as it's something we find acceptable. Don't push us, and we won't push you. Yet.

Anne spent a little longer with Jennings performing the mental hand holding necessary at this time to help foster the bond between handler and agent. However, her heart was not in it. There was someone she was far keener to see. She made her goodbyes presently, then headed out of the door and went to the next room. When she saw him sat down eating a bowl of cereal, she smiled deeply. Geoff looked up, spoon halfway to his mouth, which cracked open a smile full of half chewed food.

"Hey man," breathed Anne. She sat down on the same sofa, careful to leave plenty of space between them.

"Hello," said the teacher. Anne wondered at that description. He may not teach anymore, maybe never again. Yet he probably thought of himself as a teacher more now than ever before. She felt proud to have been a part of that process. She was also glad she got to move him out of the limelight. She had seen how innocent people handle public scrutiny and this would have been way above and beyond the call of duty. Still, he was not, technically, anyone's actual prisoner.

"How do you feel about going home?"

Geoff laughed wearily at that. "I don't really fancy being The Most Dangerous Man in The World."

"Come on, you know that's not true."

"Yeah, so do you. But I'm still here in this room, wherever this is. No, don't tell me. I don't think I could do another lie right now. If I'm not The Most Dangerous, I am definitely the Most Hated. I brought aliens to Earth and I helped them murder soldiers. I have no job. No prospects. And I am not sure my parents would be glad to have me back around the house."

Anne thought of Geoff's parents and how they had handled the press who had tracked them down. The mother had wept at the loss of privacy whilst the father had defended his son and denounced the paparazzi as 'scumbags who deserved a long, slow death.' Anne did not tell Geoff this. It was important for her that he felt isolated on all fronts. He was her friend but he was also the sole point of contact with the Alien Designate Blue. She stood up and walked around the room.

"Well, you are a welcome guest of Uncle Sam, free to leave whenever you want to. You have all the TV you need and all the Internet at your disposal. There are no security cameras in here; you have complete privacy twenty-four hours a day. You can order anything to eat or drink on the phone."

"And all you want from me is?"

"Blue. They want Blue. They need to know what he knows. They need to know what else is out there."

"You mean the City."

"Who lives there? What do they want? What does their existence mean for us and vice versa?

"I don't know that stuff."

"Blue does. Where's Blue, Geoff? Where's Blue?" As if her words were a trigger, which of course they were, with the cereal being the truth

153

agent, or rather the truth serum contained in the milk, Geoff's eyes became placid. He replied in a monotone voice.

"I don't know. If I knew I would never tell you."

Anne pursed her lips. Luckily the same truth serum would act as a short term amnesiac. He would finish his cereal presently and think he had daydreamed whilst watching the news. She got up to leave.

Then something extraordinary happened. Geoff's eyes dilated, his pupils becoming huge dark discs on a par with Blue's set. He spoke to himself as if Anne was not even in the room.

"Blue? Blue? It's you! You're alive! Where are you? Why is it so dark? Yes, I'm fine. No, they are helping me. I know, it's a cage. But I want to be in it for a while. It's a safe place. Why am I talking? They put something in my food. I can't think so well right now. What are you doing?"

Geoff's head was filled with imagery, movement and Geoff knew instinctively, naturally, perfectly, that what he was seeing was from Blue's perspective. Blue was hiding behind some construction girders. Behind him, Geoff could feel the tarpaulin rub against his fur. He knew what it meant to have fur. Revelation of the senses gave way to the action unfolding before him. The Rift may have been hidden within the giant work-tent but inside that tent, Blue's home-world continued to exist. As Blue watched it carefully, Geoff watched with him.

A series of figures appeared on the other side of the Rift. They were looking out, which meant that they were really looking in. Some were huge, gray blobs, while others were slight and yet tall. All took their time with the border of the Rift. As Blue/Geoff watched, one rose into the air, arms held out to the side as a form of grotesque balance. It touched the Rift in the sky and seemed pleased with the result.

The group of beings stopped at the same time and retreated back. Now they could not be so easily seen by Blue. He almost started forward when he saw him. A giant of a man, all made of shadow. It wore no clothes, had no features. The creature of shadow looked at the other beasts then stepped through the portal. As he did so, the creature's form changed. White, translucent skin, delicate features similar to a human but with faint scarring forming beautiful whorl patterns. Only the eyes remained charcoal black. Clothes formed from seemingly nothing, covering him in an elegant but quite dated suit. Blue pressed himself to the girder in fear. The fear gripped Geoff and, in the presence of Anne, he wept and wailed.

"He's here! He's here!"

The Shadow stood still on Earth for a moment, sniffing the air and cocking his head slowly around the entire area. He smiled.

Geoff's eyes returned to normal and he stared at Anne hard.

"We have a problem."

About the Author

David Mansell was raised in Watford, and lived in Korea. He's a husband and father, and proud to be both. He's also a noted face-licker, and will happily drop everything to lose a dance battle. A freestyle MC of cringe worthy renown, and occasionally he writes things. He loves it, and you.

More from Pondicherry Books

The Mystical Bathhouse – Doyoon Lee
Minho lives a typical, mundane life. Then one day he walks into a nondescript bathhouse on the edge of Seoul and his life is flipped upside down. In the depths of a bottomless bath, Minho's wildest fantasies seem to come true. With the help of a Turkish chef, a hard-partying Russian businessman, and a Hawaiian Punch-addicted mystery woman named X, Minho will have to rethink everything he believed to be possible and true. Will he succeed in navigating a world so absurd, or will the chaos eat him alive?

The Nana Trilogy – Serena Ishii
Meet Nana, a mute vagabond who travels Japan by bicycle and performs a street theater show known as kamishibai. Her three act performance is the strangest thing Kentaro (a middle-aged office worker) has ever seen. But something about it intrigues him, and after the show, he finds himself sitting face-to-face with Nana in a coffee shop on the edge of Osaka. Is her story make-believe? Is it possible that every scene in her kamishibai is, in fact, true? Kentaro must find out for himself.

The Rowdy and the Reckless – Su Weon Park
A dysfunctional family is struggling to keep their failing restaurant afloat in a small Korean town. When a crew of construction workers start to show up every day for lunch, Granny Maria thinks her prayers have been answered, but the construction crew is loud, dirty and rude. Grandpa Kwon, the zen one in the family, can't stand the headache their new clientele is causing him. Tempers flare between Granny Maria, Grandpa Kwon, and their two adult children, who are only in town to hide out from their own troubles. Rumors circulate about a potentially priceless ancient relic discovered by a young Vietnamese worker on the construction site. The family is willing to go to any lengths to get their hands on this relic, even if it means turning against each other.

Visit www.pondicherrybooks.webnode.com for more information.